BETWEEN
THE
HEAD
AND
THE
HANDS

BETWEEN THE HEAD AND THE HANDS

JAMES CHAARANI

Published by ECW Press
665 Gerrard Street East
Toronto, Ontario, Canada M4M 1Y2
416-694-3348 / info@ecwpress.com

Editor for the Press: Pia Singhal
Copy-editor: Jen Knoch
Cover design: Caroline Suzuki
Front cover image: Serhii Tyaglovsky / Unsplash

LIBRARY AND ARCHIVES CANADA CATALOGUING
IN PUBLICATION

Title: Between the head and the hands / James
Chaarani.

Names: Chaarani, James, author.

Identifiers: Canadiana (print) 20230457754 |
Canadiana (ebook) 20230458734

ISBN 978-1-77041-668-0 (softcover)
ISBN 978-1-77852-185-0 (ePub)
ISBN 978-1-77852-186-7 (PDF)
ISBN 978-1-77852-187-4 (Kindle)

Subjects: LCGFT: Novels.

Classification: LCC PS8605.H2 B48 2023 | DDC
C813/.6—dc23

This book is funded in part by the Government of Canada. *Ce livre est financé en partie par le gouvernement du Canada.* We acknowledge the support of the Canada Council for the Arts. *Nous remercions le Conseil des arts du Canada de son soutien.* We acknowledge the funding support of the Ontario Arts Council (OAC), an agency of the Government of Ontario. We also acknowledge the support of the Government of Ontario through the Ontario Book Publishing Tax Credit, and through Ontario Creates.

PRINTED AND BOUND IN CANADA   PRINTING: MARQUIS   5   4   3   2   1

1

When he told her he was gay Michael's mom, Samira, said he'd never live a normal life. She asked, "Are you going to change, or are you going to be a faggot?" When she said "faggot," it sounded like it was the first time she'd ever used the word. Maybe it was; she'd probably only ever heard it used on TV. It didn't sound right coming from her mouth. It was like she wasn't sure she could say it, but once she had, it was a lot easier for her to say it again: "Faggot! Is that what you're going to be? I won't have a faggot living in this house!"

She'd somehow learned the word even though her English wasn't great. It was a word that meant more than just being gay. It meant non-Muslim, non-Arab. Maybe he was ajnabi? When Michael was a kid, they'd go to Lebanon on vacation for a month or two, and his cousins who lived there, who he hardly knew, would call him that. They'd say he had a funny accent when he spoke Arabic too. They'd laugh and tell him to repeat words he'd mispronounced like he was dumb. He'd laugh with them even though he hated being teased like that. They'd use big words around him and speak really fast to see if he could understand, which he usually couldn't, not when they were going fast. He was born in Canada, so his Arabic was basic. He couldn't read or write it either, just speak and only sort of. They didn't seem to trust him for it.

Michael went downstairs to the laundry room and grabbed a suitcase from behind the washer. He was calmer than he thought he'd be, telling himself that this was how it had to be. It was fate; there was no reason to get worked up over it.

His mom was still leaning against the doorframe of his bedroom when he came back up. She had this look like she'd been punched in the gut. Michael went past, pretending that she wasn't even there. It was the way things needed to be.

He'd always told himself that if his parents asked if he was gay, he'd say yes. She asked, so he said yes. He got it in his head that if he was honest about it, things would turn out in the end, like the world was simple like that. He didn't even cry in front of her; he was able to keep it all in by taking deep breaths. His whole body was full of tears, but he wouldn't let any of it show.

He packed his favourite clothes, his school textbooks, and a notepad and dragged the suitcase down the stairs. His mother followed quietly like a cat. He couldn't even hear her, but she was behind him. She stopped at the second-last stair facing the front door. She stood there, stunned, and when she started to cry, Michael thought she was going to take it all back, everything that she'd said, but she didn't. She didn't try to stop him when he opened the front door either, or when he closed it behind him, which surprised him a bit.

He dragged his suitcase through the empty streets after midnight, trying to keep pace with his belief that this was the right thing to do. There weren't any cars on the road. It was just him, the buzzing sound from the lamppost on the street, and his suitcase wheels skipping over the grooves in the sidewalk, scratching the concrete.

It was spitting rain, but after dragging the bag for a bit, it started pouring. Michael laughed at his luck as he ploughed through the rain smacking the road. It took everything in him to keep going even though he had nowhere to go. He'd been a bit of a loner growing up so he had nobody to call. At least nobody he wanted to call, and his phone battery had died an hour before his mom asked him all that stuff.

He ended up at a gas station at the end of their subdivision. He went in, and the kid behind the counter started laughing at Michael. He and his suitcase were drenched. The kid pointed and said, "You got kicked out, didn't you?" He made it sound like it happened all the time.

"Yeah." Michael was about to laugh, but he almost broke down in tears. "Can I use your telephone? My phone died."

o

Michael had spoken to Mr. Pence for the first time on a hookup app a few months before this. Pence had taught history and English at the high school Michael had graduated from. He never had him as his teacher, but he'd see him around and remembered some students saying he was gay, that he had a boyfriend, and they lived together. He was the first gay person Michael had seen outside of TV or the movies.

When Michael would walk by him at school, he used to get nervous, believing that Pence would know that he was gay just by looking at him like he had a sixth sense. He'd forget how to walk: his feet would get heavy, and he'd have to remind himself to move each leg, left then right.

Pence wasn't handsome; he'd admit it. He had wavy blond and grey hair and always wore turtlenecks with some vest that made his head look too big for his body. Michael thought about him so much that he'd confused fascination with attraction and developed a crush on him.

When he saw him on the gay app, he said hello right away, admitting that he recognized him from his high school. He told him that he'd graduated last year.

I'm in my first semester at Waterloo, he wrote.

Thanks for the message, Pence wrote back. *Do you have a pic?*

Michael's profile was mostly blank; he wouldn't dare post a picture of himself, not like Pence, who had a photo of himself in front of a Christmas tree with shiny ornaments hanging off it.

Nobody knows I'm gay, Michael said.

Sorry but I need to know who I'm talking to.

Nobody knows I'm gay, Michael said again.

I need a pic.

Michael's phone was flat on his bedroom desk. He was huddled over it, waiting for another message to come through from Pence, hoping he'd give in. He kept flicking his finger across the screen to refresh the page, but it seemed like the conversation was done.

He'd never seen Pence on the app before and worried if he didn't send something he wouldn't see him again. He started going through the photos on his phone and found one of himself rollerblading. He didn't have his shirt on in it; it was tucked into his back pocket and he had a backwards cap on. He looked different than he normally looked because he never wore caps, but it had been really sunny that day.

Before Michael could talk himself out of it, he pressed Send and wrote, *My life is in your hands.*

Pence wrote back right away and said he recognized him from school but never would have thought he was gay. He asked Michael which classes he'd taken and the teachers he had. When he mentioned his eleventh-grade English teacher, Mr. Taylor, Pence said he was a "big homo" and a "closet case." Michael didn't get it or know how to respond other than by saying, *I don't know.*

They chatted online a couple of more times before deciding to meet at a coffee shop close to the university in Waterloo. When Michael got there, Pence was sitting by the window with his back to the door reading a paper.

That same feeling Michael got in his stomach when he'd see Pence in high school came right back. It made him sick, so he didn't say hello right away. He walked to the front counter and looked up at the menu board even though he knew what he wanted. He finally said, "A regular coffee, please," but it didn't sound right coming out of his mouth—it was like someone else was saying it. When he passed the bill over the counter, he noticed his hands were shaking, which made them shake more.

He turned around with his cup of coffee, which felt heavy in his hand. Too heavy, like he was going to drop it. He considered leaving—Pence still had his face in the paper and wouldn't notice—but Michael told himself that he needed to do this.

He took a deep breath and started walking to him. He found himself standing over Pence for a second before he said, "Hi."

"Michael?" Pence looked up from the newspaper and removed his glasses. "Wow, you're more handsome than I remember."

"You doing good?" Michael asked.

"Better now."

"Good."

"Please. Sit down."

Michael put his body above the chair and dropped.

"How are you?"

"Just got out of class."

Silence.

"Did you tell me what you're studying?"

"Major in marketing," Michael said. "Minor in literature." A single stream of sweat started trickling down the left side of his face. Pence noticed it and watched it fall.

"Marketing and literature?"

"Yeah." Silence. "I don't—" He shook his head.

"You don't?"

"I don't think I told you."

"I don't think you did. Are you enjoying it?"

"It's cool. We have to read books really fast. For English, I mean—the English courses. Sometimes we have to read a book a day. I don't like that. I love everything else. I am happy with what I'm studying."

"A book a day?" Pence whistled softly and seemed impressed.

"It's crazy."

"Are you from Kitchener? You must be if you went to my school."

Michael told him that he was born and raised there, yeah, but his parents were from Lebanon and came during the war. He went on about how he wasn't a fan of the city and would've rather gone to university somewhere bigger, but his parents made too much money for him to get a student loan but not enough to send him away to school so he was stuck.

"Well, I'm glad you're stuck," Pence said. "We wouldn't have met if you left."

Michael was relieved when Pence asked if he wanted to go back to his place and continue talking over a glass of wine. He hated sitting there with someone who looked so gay.

Pence lived in a large yellow-brick farmhouse past the last subdivision at the city limits on a quiet country road. There was nothing else around except for massive forests and cornfields. It was an old place that creaked when they walked through the front door. Every step had a new sound. Michael was expecting it to be more rustic inside, but the furniture was a mix of old and new, mismatched without much thought. The place was cluttered with books, papers, file folders, and magazines.

Pence opened a bottle of red wine and served crackers with orange cheddar he'd nuked in the microwave. The cheese blotched on top like sponge toffee.

They sat on the sofa in the living room with their thighs touching. It embarrassed Michael to be so close. It felt like it was his fault that they were close, so he pushed his legs together as much as he could.

"Are you okay?" Pence said. He didn't seem worried either way. Michael nodded but didn't say anything.

"It's okay. Relax. It's fine. Have a drink." Pence handed him his glass that had been sitting on the coffee table. "Cheers."

"Cheers."

"I got this wine from a shop in Niagara. Do you like wine?"

"Yeah, it's good."

"You like this one?"

He took another sip. "It's good." He didn't know good wine from bad but wanted to stop talking about himself. "How long have you lived here?"

Pence put his hand on Michael's thigh, but Michael started worrying it'd make him hard. He didn't want to get hard, not like that.

"You seem tense," Pence said.

Michael tried to laugh, but he was feeling very tense. "I'm fine."

"Okay, okay. Well, I've been here for twelve years. Now finish up your drink and let me get you another."

Michael downed the half glass he had left.

"Do you like Sade?" Pence said.

"What's that?"

"The musician."

Michael laughed for real this time. "I thought it was a drink."

"Please tell me you've heard of Sade."

"Maybe."

"Maybe? Well, let me introduce you to Sade." He left the room and a moment later music started playing from the speaker in the corner of the room. Michael had heard the song before, maybe from when he was a kid. It was possible his mom listened to it; he was sure he'd heard it somewhere.

Pence came back with two glasses of wine nearly filled to the top.

"It's not Britney Spears or Gaga—this is when music was good."

"I've heard this before. I didn't know who it was, but I've heard it."

"Well, thank god," Pence said. "Or Allah or whoever." He laughed. "Cheers."

Michael was glad when he sat down next to him and put his hand back on his thigh again. He was still nervous about getting hard, but it made it feel like they were boyfriends too, like there was something between them.

He drank more wine and listened to Pence talk about the house some more, how he was supposed to renovate it before his ex had moved out and how he was ready to get going with it again. He needed to find a contractor first.

"I've started dating again, obviously," he said. "For a long time, I couldn't date. I couldn't do anything. I need to get this place fixed up."

Michael wondered whether he was going to renovate his house for him. He wasn't sure but liked the thought of it.

He had more wine and leaned back into the sofa, relaxing his body for the first time. He focused on Pence's lips while he kept talking about how he was going to renovate his place. He knew he could kiss him if he wanted to. Pence wouldn't stop him. He'd never kissed anybody, not like the way he wanted to kiss Pence but he knew he could.

"You're sure you're okay?" Pence said.

"You keep asking me that."

"Just making sure."

"How did you know you were gay?" Michael said.

"I was always gay. You're born gay, don't forget that."

Had Michael always been gay, even when he was a kid? It was hard for him to think exactly when he started feeling like this. He was young but always? Even as a baby?

"I was engaged—did you know that?" Pence asked.

"No. Did you tell me?"

"I can't remember."

14

"I didn't know."

"I was."

"To a man?"

"*Her*," he said, letting it settle in, "her name was Sylvia. Does that surprise you?"

Michael blushed and picked up a cracker.

"Surprised you, didn't I?"

Michael shrugged and said, "I don't know," which made Pence laugh so hard he had to put his drink down so it wouldn't spill. He started rubbing Michael's thigh like he was trying to console him.

"I scared you," he said. "Oh no!"

"No."

"I did. You should see the look on your face!"

Michael blushed. "What happened with her?"

"I called it off, obviously, a week before the wedding. I told the poor thing I was gay. She was devastated," he said, rolling his eyes. "Apparently I ruined her life. She said I must've known the whole time, which I did." He chuckled.

"Do you still talk?"

The way he raised his eyebrows made Michael feel stupid for asking. "Of course not. I ruined her life." He chuckled again but then became serious. "I wish we could've been friends. I liked her. We were friends, but she just couldn't accept me being a homo, I guess."

Michael reached for another cracker, and Pence took one too.

When the next Sade song came on, Pence closed his eyes and hummed along. It was a love ballad; it didn't sound as old as the other one. It sounded kind of new. Michael hadn't heard it, but he didn't mind the song.

Pence opened his eyes to Michael watching him. "Did I tell you how beautiful you are?"

Michael turned red again. "Yeah."

"I want to kiss you so bad."

"I want to kiss you too."

"Then kiss me, stupid."

Pence's lips were salty from the crackers, and his mouth had a strange taste. It was something Michael had tasted before but he couldn't tell what it was. He didn't think too much about that though. Instead, he moved his lips the way he thought he should, up and down, with his tongue sticking right out. It was a sloppy kiss, but Pence was nothing but grateful.

At one point, Michael placed his hands on either side of Pence's face while they kissed and thought how his cheeks felt softer than they looked, kind of loose, like they weren't a part of him. Michael got embarrassed when his erection started to push against his jeans, so he tried to hide it, but Pence said, "That's normal. When you're kissing another guy, you're supposed to get a boner."

It was weird for Michael to hear him say "boner." He used to say it around his friends when he was younger, but he hadn't heard it since then. Maybe Pence picked it up from his students.

Pence took Michael's shirt off and ran his hand across his chest. "You're so beautiful," he said. "I have to admit, I have a thing for Arabs." He stood him up and turned him around to get a better look. "Come with me."

Pence led Michael to the upstairs bathroom. "I want to show you something." Beside the shower was a ladder that led up to a loft. Pence started climbing, and halfway up, he turned his head and said, "Come on."

The first thing Michael saw was a bunch of patchwork pillows covering the floor like a Moroccan den. Then he noticed dildos, butt plugs, and lubricants.

"Don't worry, I won't be using those on you," Mr. Pence said, picking up one of the dildos that was the length of his forearm. He laughed the same way he did when he was talking about his ex-fiancé, Sylvia.

The ceiling wasn't high enough for them to stand up, so Pence crawled to the far side of the loft and said, "Come here." When Michael got close, he pulled him in and started kissing him again. They fell into the pillows and took their clothes off. Michael had never felt another guy's body up against his, but it was like nothing else.

Michael didn't know how to give a blowjob and gagged a few times since Pence's dick was really big and bumpy. It had a smell to it too and tasted funny. His teeth got in the way, which made Pence jump, but after he got over the pain, he moaned and reminded Michael how beautiful he was.

o

Michael returned to Pence's a bunch more times, but they didn't just screw around. They'd hang out, talking about movies or books and sometimes Michael would bring up what he was learning in class. He'd been reading *Manufacturing Consent* by Noam Chomsky and would go on about that one the most, saying how untrustworthy the mass media was, how it was all just business for profit. Pence joked that Michael was a paranoid socialist when he went on about that, and it became something they liked to laugh about together.

Some nights if Pence had some marking to do, Michael would sit at the table with him and study. They'd have dinner then he'd go back home at the time he'd normally go back anyway—if he wasn't studying there he'd be in the library so his parents wouldn't know the difference.

Pence started teaching him how to cook chicken, pork, or whatever he was making for them each night, and before dinner they'd always have a glass of wine and crackers with cheddar nuked on top like they did that first time. It became Michael's job to get that ready and pick out the wine.

Michael's birthday fell on a Saturday, but Pence wanted to do something special for him the Thursday before. It was the only day Michael could get away because his mom invited family over on Friday and Saturday for his birthday. Pence picked up some fresh ravioli from an Italian shop and made his own pasta sauce. He was going to get some special cheese too to start, but Michael said he wanted to do their regular cheddar on crackers in the microwave. He didn't need anything fancy.

That night, Pence got the candles going on the table while they ate and burned a CD—Michael didn't think that people still did that. It had a couple of Sade songs on it, and some Whitney Houston, Lionel Richie, and a few artists Michael didn't know. They were all slow songs though and made it feel like they were in a restaurant. It was the only time Michael would hear songs like that, which Pence said was the point of it. He said he'd normally take him out somewhere but he didn't want people to get the wrong idea. "They'd probably just think you're my son anyway," he said. "But just in case we run into someone from the school."

When they finished dinner, Pence went to the bathroom but told Michael not to go into the fridge, making him promise that he wouldn't. Michael figured that's where the cake was, so he promised because he wanted to be surprised. He started clearing the plates and cutlery off the table and putting them in the kitchen sink. When he went back for another bottle of wine, the doorbell rang.

"Should I get it?" he shouted. "Peter? Do you want me to get the door?" It rang again. "I'm going to get it," he said. "Peter?"

The man on the other side of the door seemed confused to see Michael standing there. He was short but stocky with dark hair that nearly covered his eyes. "Who are you?" he said, pushing his hair to the side.

"I'm a friend."

"Is Peter here?"

"He's just in the bathroom." Michael turned his head and shouted, "There's someone at the door for you!" Michael waited a second, looking back into the house, but Pence didn't answer.

"How old are you?" the man asked.

"Nineteen. On Saturday. Almost nineteen."

"Oh. Happy birthday."

"Do you want to come in?"

"I should wait here."

"Okay, I'll see where he is."

Michael left the door open and went back into the house. "Peter?" he said. He went to the stairs and shouted again, "Peter?"

"Who's at the door?"

"A man. I don't know."

Pence came down the stairs in a different shirt. It was navy blue, tucked into his corduroy pants. He'd never seen him dressed up like that with his shirt tucked in. It looked like he put some water through his hair too.

"He's at the door still?"

"I think so."

"What does he want?"

"I don't know."

"The cake is in the fridge. Take it out—it's better at room temperature. I'll be right there."

"Okay."

"Just stay in the kitchen."

Michael did as he was told. Whatever was happening, it had nothing to do with him, and he wanted to see what cake he got. He could see through the window in the box that it was a Black Forest, his favourite kind. He couldn't remember whether he told Pence that. It could've been a coincidence, or maybe he did tell him.

He opened the box on the counter and wondered whether Pence got candles and was going to sing "Happy Birthday." He never liked having "Happy Birthday" sung to him, getting all that attention, but he liked the cake.

"I'll mail it to you," he heard Pence say, coming back into the house. "No, no, no—you think I've just been holding on to it? I haven't had a chance to throw it out yet, so don't flatter yourself. No, I said I'll mail it to you. You're not coming in the house and don't come by here again." He slammed the door.

When he came into the kitchen, Michael waited for him to say something about what had happened, but Pence was talking to himself. He was acting like Michael wasn't even there.

"Thanks for the cake," Michael said. He didn't know what else to say.

Pence jumped, startled by Michael's voice. "Oh. You're very welcome," he said, noticing him then. "It's nice to be appreciated."

He waited for him to say more but he didn't, so Michael opened another bottle of wine instead and poured himself a glass. "Do you want some more?"

"Do I have a temper?"

He had to think about the question; it wasn't what he thought he was going to say. "I don't think so."

He threw his right arm up. "Well, thank you. See?" He turned to the front door like the guy was still standing there. "You're the one with the temper, thank you."

Michael poured Pence some wine; it seemed that he needed it.

"I'm glad you got to finally meet Rodel. I knew the day would come."

"Who is he?"

"My ex. He used to live here."

"I didn't know that."

"He said I have a temper." He looked back at the door. "Maybe I wouldn't have such a temper if you weren't such a bad person." He threw both arms up this time. "He makes me this way. This isn't me."

Michael looked down at his drink; he didn't think he should be there. Whatever was happening felt private, and he suddenly wanted to go home. "Do you want me to leave?"

"Of course not."

"If you change your mind, just say so."

"Of course not, don't be stupid. It's your birthday"

"Sorry." Silence. "What did he want?"

"He has some clothes here. I put it all in the attic because I didn't think he was coming back. Honestly, I was going to throw it out but didn't have time. I forgot it was even there."

Michael felt like asking him about the cake again, thinking it might change how everything felt. He wanted things to go back to the way they were before.

"I don't like talking about Rodel," he said. "I wasn't trying to keep his stuff. I put it in the attic so I wouldn't think about it. I didn't want to see him; that's why I wasn't answering his calls. I didn't want to see him. Now he comes to my door." He started crying. Michael had never seen someone cry in real life because of something like this. He'd seen it on TV a bunch of times, people crying about a breakup, but never in person. He felt like he was supposed to hug him and say things to make him stop crying, but he just stared at him. "He ruined my life. You know, I broke up with him," Pence said. "I broke up," he said again. "He was cheating on me. I caught him having sex in our own bed upstairs. The same one. I came home from school early and caught them fucking. What a fuckin' cliché. I thought that only happened on TV."

Pence grabbed his wine and drank it in one gulp. He wiped the tears from his face and poured himself some more. "It was a fuckin' melodrama. And you think he'd say sorry. Nope. Nope, he left that night and moved in with fuckface. A teacher who transferred from Halifax. That's who he was fucking."

Michael wanted to leave but couldn't figure out how so he grabbed a knife and started cutting the cake. If Pence had planned on putting candles on it or singing "Happy Birthday," he didn't say anything.

"How did you know this is my favourite cake?"

"You told me last week," Pence said, but he seemed annoyed by the question. "It's a good thing you're pretty. Don't you remember telling me?"

He didn't, but he said that he did now because he felt stupid for forgetting.

"It's a good thing you're pretty," he said again. It seemed to make him feel better to say it, to laugh at Michael.

Michael thought that there'd be a gift after the cake but there wasn't. Pence made him dinner and got the cake, that was it. Michael didn't show that he was disappointed.

o

When they had sex later on, Michael noticed that Pence had a smell to him that he hadn't smelled before. It wasn't some skunky body odour. It came from all over; it was like unripe bananas. When he got home that night, he could smell it on his fingers, and even after washing his hands, he could smell it.

He smelled it the next time they had sex too. It was all he could smell; it was exactly like unripe bananas.

He tried having sex with him once more to see if the smell came back. When it did he decided that he didn't want to do this anymore. The smell made him wonder whether he ever really liked Pence or if it was just about having sex with a guy—any guy.

He decided to stop calling him. Pence had other people he screwed around with anyway, so Michael figured it was fine to disappear and blocked him from his phone.

A couple of weeks later when Michael was studying for a midterm in his room, his mom shouted that there was a man on the phone for him. He could hear her listening in on the other end when he picked up. "I got it, Mom." She still didn't put the phone down. "Mom, I got it!"

Michael had always called Pence from his cell. Pence shouldn't have had his home phone but he did.

Pence started apologizing and said that he didn't want to call. He made it out like he was worried about him and thought something bad had happened. That's the only reason he called.

"They don't know about me," Michael whispered. "Why would you call?"

Mr. Pence said he was sorry again, that he was just worried. He was glad that he was okay, that nothing bad had happened.

He asked where he'd been. Michael said he was busy with school. It was exam time. "I can't talk now. Don't call here again. I'll call you."

But he didn't call. He found a way to block his number on the home phone too, but the next week Pence showed up at his university, waiting outside one of the lecture halls he used to drop Michael off at. Michael probably shouldn't have been surprised to see him, but he was surprised.

Pence was pacing, saying stuff to himself before seeing Michael there.

"What are you doing?" Michael whispered.

"You said you'd call."

Michael pulled him to the side of the building, away from everyone. "Why did you call me at home? You know that my parents don't know."

"You disappeared."

"I told you I have exams. I have one in ten minutes."

"You could still have called. Ever since Rodel—"

"I'm sick of hearing about Rodel. It's annoying."

"I didn't know you felt that way. I'm sorry. I'm sorry. I can stop talking about him."

"I don't want you as my boyfriend."

"I never said we're boyfriends."

"Okay."

Silence.

"So, what? You're not gay now?" All of a sudden, Pence wasn't as anxious. He got serious, kind of condescending. "I was just an experiment?"

"That's not what I said," he whispered.

"Michael, I miss you. We always had such a good time together."

"I'm not interested in you. Sexually, I mean." He'd never felt that mature before, stating a sexual preference. He was learning what he liked and didn't like and was able to be clear about it. It made him feel like a grown-up.

Pence grabbed his arm and said, "Please, Michael."

Whatever pride Michael felt about this newfound maturity quickly turned to pity. Pence was the first gay guy Michael had known, but he was also the first gay guy he'd seen like this.

"I have to go. I have an exam right now. I'll call you tonight. I promise." It strained his face to smile but he smiled. "Let's go for a coffee tomorrow."

Pence squeezed his arm. "I'm sorry I'm like this."

Michael thought about him during the exam and the hours after. Begrudgingly, he did call him, and they met for coffee the next night. They went to the same place they'd first met because that's what Pence wanted.

He was trying to be upbeat, saying how good Michael looked, but he also made backhanded comments about how he'd just disappeared. Michael wasn't sure how to react, so he ignored it and talked about how he thought he did on some of his exams.

After their coffees, Pence invited him back to his place for some wine and crackers for old times' sake. Michael said that he needed to study and that they should just be friends.

"Am I that bad?" Pence said, but before Michael could answer, he continued, "I'm just joking. I get it."

o

Pence was the very last person he wanted to call from the gas station after being kicked out. He'd avoided him for weeks, but standing there soggy with his suitcase and the kid behind the counter still laughing, Michael dialled him up on the gas station phone.

Pence sounded surprised to hear from him but happy too.

"Oh, Michael, I'm so sorry," he said when he heard what had happened.

He arrived at the gas station a half-hour later and apologized again but acted like everything was fine between them, like Michael hadn't been avoiding him.

"What made you decide to come out tonight, you crazy boy?"

"I didn't."

"Well, you must've."

"My mom just asked if I was gay. I said yes. I was waiting though."

"For what?"

"Until I finish school and get a job, so I'm not in this situation. I should've said no."

"Tell me what happened."

o

Pence took Michael's suitcase down to the basement. It was unfinished, with concrete floors that had huge cracks zigzagging from the drains. There was pink fibreglass coming out from the wooden frames of the walls and light bulbs dangling from the ceiling. It was cold down there, damp and musty.

"You can stay here as long as you need to," Pence said.

There was a bed in the far corner with a desk next to it. Pence leaned over and smelled the sheets. "Stupid cat," he said. "I need to change these. There's pee everywhere. I'll be back." He went upstairs.

Michael put his bag down on the ground and moved the desk closer to the bed, getting it set up how he liked. Pence noticed the desk moved when he came back down and told him to do whatever he wanted down there.

"Get the other side," he said, removing the old sheets and laying down the clean ones. "I wish I had something nicer for you, but it's a comfortable bed. I sleep down here in the summers when it gets too hot."

He started feeling guilty for how he'd treated Pence before. He thought he should say something about it while they fixed up the bed. It was nice to let him stay and get him sheets like that, nice he didn't make a big deal of how Michael stopped calling before. He wanted to say sorry and was about to, but he didn't have the energy. Why talk about what happened before, anyway? That's what he thought. Everything before seemed like it was before and now it was different. Before didn't matter. He didn't want it to matter. This was a new life. That was old, and all he cared about was now, anyway.

"Is this okay?" Pence said when the sheets were changed.

"Yeah."

"Are you sure?"

"Yeah."

"You've had a night."

"I know," he said. He laughed for a second but then he started to cry—it just came out. He didn't plan it. He didn't like it either. "Why am I crying?" he said, wiping his eyes with his sleeve.

"It's okay, silly boy. You're allowed to cry. Come here."

He let Pence squeeze him and he cried some more. "I don't know why I'm crying," he kept saying, like it wasn't him doing it, like it was someone else doing it to him.

"You've been through it," Pence said. "Let it out. You'll be fine if you just let it out. You'll get to the other side."

"I'm sorry."

"Don't be sorry. It's fine. I'm going to take care of you. I promise."

o

There was a clothes rack on wheels near the washing machine in the basement, which Michael carted over. He took his shirts out from his bag and hung them, using the rack to make a wall at the foot of the bed so it felt more like a room. Pence had gone upstairs, but he figured he'd be okay with him using the rack. There was nothing on it anyway.

He took his books out too and stood them up along a wood ledge in the unfinished wall. He placed his notepads on the ledge under it, using the wall as a bookshelf. He wished he had his posters and more of his books to make it feel like home, but he figured he could go and buy more posters on the weekend if he still felt like it.

He didn't realize how tired he was until he laid down on the bed. He couldn't remember falling asleep and woke up the next day. It was hard to tell the time down there. There were two tiny windows, but they were on the other side of the basement near the dryer. Enough light was coming in that he knew it was morning. Even though he didn't have any dreams, it felt like he had slept a long time.

He reached for his phone in his pocket, but then he remembered he left it upstairs in the kitchen when they'd come in. He got out of bed to go look for it.

The sun was coming in from the bottom of the basement door as he went up the stairs. It was blinding when he opened the door, with sunlight coming in through the front window and bouncing off the ceramic floors.

"Peter?" he whispered. His voice was eaten up by the silence so he said it even louder: "Peter?"

He thought that he put his phone on the kitchen counter, but it wasn't there. He walked all around the kitchen island looking for it.

"Peter?" he said, raising his voice to a near shout.

He tried to remember what day it was but he couldn't. He knew it wasn't Monday. It couldn't be Friday—it was midweek sometime—maybe Tuesday or Wednesday. He wondered whether Pence had already gone to work. "Peter, are you home?"

The clock behind him went off with a half bell. It made him jump. The sound filled in the silence, but it got quiet again.

He turned. It was eight-thirty. Pence would've had to be at school by now. "Peter?" he said. "Are you home?"

He'd never been in Pence's place without him. It made it feel like he was somewhere else, like it was a different place. Everything looked the same but different; it was defined by Pence's presence. The sofa, the big clock, everything just looked like stuff that only Pence would own.

He found his phone on the side table by the front door, but it was dead. He kept pressing at it but nothing happened, and he remembered it'd died the night before, and he forgot his charger back at his parent's place. Pence had the same type of phone though. Michael helped him pick it not that long after they'd met. He figured Pence would have a charger around somewhere, so he started looking around in the living room and dining room. He got on his knees and checked all the wall sockets, but he couldn't find it. He looked in the kitchen too, but there was nothing.

He went upstairs to Pence's bedroom and stuck his head in. "Peter?" he said before going in. The bed was made and the room tidy. There was nothing on the dresser or side tables. There was no dust anywhere either. He must've just cleaned it, but the room still smelled like unripe bananas. The rest of the house wasn't like that, just his bedroom, and it was so heavy he began breathing out of his mouth while he looked around for a phone charger behind the dresser, next to the bed, and on the wall by the window. He checked the bathroom off the bedroom too. That's where he found it, plugged into a socket by the mirror. There was a plate next to it with half a joint snubbed out on it.

Michael plugged his phone in. He was sure there was going to be a message waiting for him from his mom. There was no way she didn't message to see where he went. But when his phone turned on, there was nothing. No text or voice mail. It bugged him enough that he blocked her number on his phone. Even if she wanted to try now, she couldn't. Whatever she had to say didn't matter; that's what he told himself. He blocked his dad's number too. If they didn't text already then they lost their chance. There weren't going to be more chances.

He turned his phone back off to let it charge. He didn't want to be in a situation where he didn't have a phone again, to have to go into a gas station to use a phone. That was stupid, he thought. He hated that.

He picked up the last bit of joint left in the plate. He put it to his lips and tried to light it with the matches next to it. It was just a roach, so the flame of the match burnt his upper lip, but he still got some smoke. He inhaled, and held it in as long as he could. That's what Pence had taught him; he said you get more high when you do that. Michael had never smoked pot before they met. Pence would have a little bit before bed every night to help him sleep. Michael would only take a drag or two, but with what was left, he was able to take four long hauls, holding them all in until he started coughing each time. It made his eyes water.

He went to sit on the toilet to take a pee and a minute later started noticing things more: the shine on the ceramic floors, the sun pouring in from the sunroof, and the grey in the granite countertops. He got up to wash his hands and ran the water. He got distracted by the sound of it. It made him smile, so he turned the water on even more. It started splashing on the counters. He'd never noticed the sound like that; there was a lot he never noticed.

He turned it off, then turned it on again. Then off and on. He started laughing at the sound it made. When he stopped doing that, turning it off for good, he admired the silence. He liked it so much he tried not to move so he wouldn't hear a thing. He didn't even breathe. It was quiet until he couldn't hold his breath anymore and that got him laughing again.

He went back downstairs and started flipping through Pence's CDs but got distracted by the sunlight coming in through the sliding door in the back. It was brighter than he'd ever seen the sun. With a CD in his hand, he went to the door and looked out into the lawn. There was a big forest past the yard that seemed to go on forever. He put his hand flat over his eyes like a visor and took a good look at the forest. It was a proper forest of mainly maple and white pine. The leaves on the maple had already turned, and most of them had fallen to the ground. Michael thought how that was probably how forests had looked thousands of years ago; it was how everything would look if people hadn't cut them all down.

Michael unlocked the sliding door and stepped out onto the grass in his socks. He thought of putting on some shoes but also thought it was kind of funny to walk on grass in his socks and liked how it felt against the bottom of his feet, kind of tickly. The grass was soaked from the storm the night before, wetting his socks, but it made him smile. He kept walking out, farther into the yard all the way to the forest. Seeing it up close made him wonder how far the forest went. He couldn't see anything on the other side but more trees.

He put his hand up and touched the trunk of the tree closest to him, planting his fingers in the ridges of the bark so it was between his knuckles. He closed his eyes to really feel it; he'd never touched one like that before.

He stepped out onto the forest floor. It was rougher and drier than the lawn; he could feel twigs breaking under his feet. It didn't hurt, but he had to move slowly. He wanted to see if he could get to the other side of the forest so he moved between trees, over large rocks and tree trunks that had toppled. Birds whistled and the wind swooshed through the pine needles above his head. The sun could barely make it through the forest because of the thickness of it, but when it did, getting in his eyes, it'd twinkle.

He found a small clearing in the middle of the forest that was right in the sun. He didn't know how long he was walking for—maybe twenty minutes—but he'd gone in deep. There was a tree stump so he sat down and took his socks off. He squeezed the water out of them and placed them on the dirt in the sun so they could dry. There was still lots of forest in front of him and all around—all he could see was trees. Pence's place was at the city limits, so he figured there really was no end to it. He didn't need to go any farther though; he was happy finding this spot. He sat out there for an hour listening to the birds. It made him smile, and he didn't think he would smile like that again, not after yesterday.

○

He walked back barefoot with his socks in his hand and used them to swat away any spiderwebs near his face. He walked even slower than before; he wished he wasn't going back to Pence's place. He didn't mind the basement. It was nice that he let him stay there, really nice—he still felt bad about how he'd ghosted him before—but he wanted his own place where he didn't owe anybody anything. He didn't know how to get a place of his own. He'd never looked into it, but he wasn't sure how long he could stay at Pence's. Maybe just a couple months until he finished the semester. It was going to go by quickly; it made the most sense to wait until the semester was over because there was already a lot going on. He just had to get through the semester, then he'd figure something out. He didn't need his own place. He could get a roommate. He wouldn't mind a roommate as long as he had his own room, so he wouldn't owe anybody anything.

○

He thought it'd be nice if he had dinner ready when Pence came back from work. He figured it was the least he could do for letting him stay in the basement for nothing, so when he got back to the house, he went through the fridge to see what he could make. He found veggies and chicken breasts. He thought maybe a stir fry would be good. Pence had taught him how to make it; he'd taught him to make lots of things, but that was probably the easiest considering what he was able to find in the fridge. He started chopping the chicken and veggies and warmed up the

31

wok with a bit of oil in it. Once it was cooked, he got a plate of crackers with cheddar on top ready and put it in the microwave. It sat in there for a couple of hours; when he saw Pence pull into the driveway he pressed the start button and put the wok back on the stove to reheat the food.

"I could get used to this," Pence said. "It smells great."

"I made dinner."

"I could tell. Thank you." He smiled. Michael wanted him to be happy and to know that he was grateful for letting him stay. "Is there anything I can do to help?"

"I couldn't find any wine."

"I keep them over here," Pence said, reaching into the side pantry. "Did you get my texts?"

"What texts?"

"I wanted to treat you to dinner."

"I made dinner though."

"I texted before I knew you made dinner."

Michael remembered that he'd blocked his phone number, that he hadn't unblocked it after they stopped talking before. He knew that was why, that he forgot to unblock him. "I haven't checked my phone today," he said. "You probably did. I just didn't check it."

"I can treat you to dinner another day," he said. "This looks delicious."

"I used whatever I could find," Michael said.

"Look, you've been through a lot. It's going to take some time."

"What is?"

"Everything. You've been through a lot, but time will make it better. I promise."

"Okay," Michael said.

"Look at me," Pence said. "I mean it. It will get better. It will. I promise."

Michael thought he could go back to class the next day. His first one was at ten, but when he woke up he didn't have it in him to pack up his bag with textbooks and try to figure out how to get to the university on the city bus. Pence had always driven him to his place, so he didn't know how to get around from there on his own. There was a bus stop down the street, but he'd never taken it, so Michael decided to skip the rest of the school week and start new on Monday. He thought the time off would be good, and he could figure out how the city buses worked between now and then.

He went upstairs to an empty house again. He assumed that Pence had already left for work; it was as quiet as it was before, but it wasn't sunny outside. The house looked dim and felt hollow without anybody there. "Peter?" he shouted. "Are you here?" He knew he wouldn't be, but he still called his name again when he went into the kitchen: "Peter?"

Pence had left some coffee for Michael, so he poured some into a travel mug and took it over to the sliding door in the back to get a look at the sky. The clouds were dark and heavy, piling up on each other. It looked cold too, with the branches of the trees in the back being pushed in the direction of the wind every few seconds. He wasn't sure if it was going to rain today. It looked like it could've, but he didn't know where his phone was to check the weather to be sure.

He grabbed his shoes and one of Pence's jackets, which was hanging by the front door, deciding to go out for a quick walk before it rained. He stepped outside and looked up at the sky again, begging whoever it was up there that was making things happen not to let it rain, at least not until he was done his walk.

He went toward the forest in the back. It didn't feel as nice as before, without the sun or without having smoked something, but at least he had his shoes on so he could go even farther into the forest if he wanted to.

When he got to the end of the yard, he stepped between the trees into the forest. It felt like entering a different country: the air was darker and there were dried leaves crunching under his feet, drier than the day before. There were no birds, just the sound of whatever it was that was cracking under his heels.

He was trying to find the clearing from yesterday, but without the sun, the forest seemed all the same. Twenty minutes in, he started to wonder whether he'd gone the wrong way and passed it altogether. Or maybe he needed to go farther. He tried to remember how long he'd walked before, but he had been high, so it was hard to tell. Everywhere he turned looked like everywhere he'd just been; any distinctness was lost without the sun's light.

He kept going deeper and got completely turned around. The forest was getting thicker with trees doubling and tripling, spinning around him. He thought of turning back, but he didn't know where back was, so he kept moving his feet, hoping for the best.

He eventually found the clearing from yesterday. "Fuck you," he said to the clearing, but he said it with love. "Fuck you, you motherfucker." He smiled and sat on the tree stump to finish his coffee. He rubbed the stump with his left hand like it was a beloved pet. It was a good spot; he couldn't explain the feeling it gave him except that he liked it and it felt like it was where he needed to be. It was somewhere just for him, a place nobody knew about but him. He wasn't going to tell anybody about it either, not even Pence. He felt he deserved something of his own.

Once he finished the coffee, he decided to tidy the area around the stump. He cleared away all the branches and sticks around it and kicked away the dried leaves. He tore a branch off a maple tree close by that had a few leaves on it and used it to sweep the ground of twigs and stones and soon it looked like something out of a fairy tale. He thought that maybe he'd look up how to make a fire pit because it'd be a nice spot for it. He could come out here when he wanted to be on his own and get a good fire going. His dad used to take him camping as a kid, and he always loved it when they'd get the fire going, the way it smelled. The clearing was big enough for one, so he thought that maybe tomorrow he'd do that.

The sun found its way out through a break in the clouds. It was like it came out of nowhere, blinding him a bit. He looked up, closed his eyes, and smiled because of how the heat felt on his face. The clearing looked even nicer in the sun with the way the light detailed everything, giving it life. The birds started singing with the sun out; it made Michael wonder if that was a thing, whether birds are more likely to sing in the sun.

He sat on the stump and felt proud of how he'd tidied the place, making it his own. The only thing he was thinking now was that he wished he had more coffee. If he had coffee it would have been perfect—he wouldn't need anything else. He considered going and making some more, but it took so long to get there, and it'd take just as long to get back. And who knows, it might be raining by then because the clouds around the sun were still heavy. He decided to just enjoy it while it lasted, whether we had more coffee or not.

He started thinking about how free he was. He hadn't thought of it until just then but before, living at home, he couldn't do what he wanted. His mom had to know about everything he did. If he went out, she'd be asking where to, always. Even if it was just to the library, she wanted to know. He couldn't go out late at night either without asking her and saying where he was going. When he was out she'd call his cell to make sure he was all right and remind him of when he said he'd come home. That was all done; he could do what he wanted now.

He didn't need to keep any more secrets about himself—he was free in that way too. Being kicked out the way he was gave him this feeling in his stomach that was still there; it was heavy and made him feel sick, but he wasn't going to get hung up on it. It seemed like a small price to pay to be free. So what if he felt a little sick?

o

Michael made more coffee when he got back to Pence's and had a bagel with peanut butter. It was the only thing he could find to eat. The fridge was empty and so were most of the cupboards, so he thought later he would try to figure out how to take the bus and go get some groceries. Pence was probably too busy with work to go get it himself, and he thought it'd be a nice thing to do.

After breakfast, he took his coffee to the living room and turned the TV on. He lay on the sofa and started playing around with the hookup app on his phone.

He started taking selfies. He wasn't happy with how they looked—the camera was too close to his face, making it seem like he had a double chin—so he got up and went over to the mirror by the fireplace. He flattened his hair and took his shirt off before taking some shots of himself in the mirror. Lots of guys had shirtless photos, and even though he was a little embarrassed by how he looked, trying to be sexier than he was, he uploaded one anyway.

Messages started coming in right away. There were so many he couldn't read them fast enough. He went through all of them, even the ones that were from guys he wasn't into; he'd talk to anyone who talked to him first, thinking it was fun because he'd never got so many messages before. Guys were telling him how good-looking he was, so he'd thank them, and they'd ask questions about him or what he liked to do in bed.

There was this one guy a couple of years older than him. His profile said he was 6'3", and he looked it in his photos. He had a big chest and wide shoulders like he played sports. He had a square jaw, and a thin beard. It said he was twenty-five but he looked thirty years old easy.

The guy said that Michael was exactly his type and asked if he was Italian.

Not Italian, Michael said. *I was born here but my parents came from Lebanon.*

That's why you're sexy, he said. *My best friend back home is Lebanese. Where is back home?*

Toronto. He told Michael that he was in Waterloo for school. He was in his last year and was going to go back to Toronto once he finished the semester. He was studying computers and already had a job lined up for when he was done.

Are you at the university too? the guy asked.

Yeah. First year.

We should meet up at school if you feel like it.

I'm actually taking the rest of the week off.

Must be nice. You need some company?

What do you mean?

You want me to come over?

Michael lied and said that his roommate was home. He couldn't have anyone over, not now. He didn't think it was a good idea to have a stranger over. And over to do what?

You can come to my place, the guy said. *My roommate is home but we can be quiet. It's a big house.*

Michael put his phone down and went into the kitchen for more coffee. He poured himself another cup, added some milk then grabbed his phone again. *I can't,* he wrote. *I gotta get groceries.*

Groceries from where?

I just moved here yesterday. I need to find somewhere to get groceries.

Where did you move to?

It's at the edge of the city. There's a bus stop close by.

Why don't you Google a grocery store?

Michael didn't even think to do that.

I've got a car, the guy wrote. *I can take you to get groceries if you don't want to take the bus.*

How do I know you're not going to kill me? he wrote. *LOL.*

You don't LOL. But you have my photo and I'll give you my number. It'd be hard for me to get away with it if you give me a call. They'd track me down.

You've thought about this.

I guess so.

LOL.

Call me, he said, giving Michael his number.

"So, you want a drive?" was the first thing he said when he picked up. His voice didn't sound how Michael thought it would. There was nothing special about it; it could've been anyone's voice and he didn't seem as confident as he did in his pictures.

"How's it going?"

"Yeah, good. So, you want a drive?"

"Sure."

The guy laughed. "Where do you live?"

"It's at the edge of the city."

"Kitchener?"

"Officially, yeah."

"Send me the address. I'll come pick you up."

"I can meet you at the bus stop down the street."

"Which bus stop?"

"There's one down the road."

"Why?"

"I'll just meet you at the bus stop. I'll send you the location."

"I just need to shower. I can be there in thirty minutes."

"Wait, what's your name?"

"Nathan. Yours?"

"Mike. Or Michael."

He laughed. "What is it? Michael or Mike?"

Michael laughed too. His face heated up.

"I'm going to call you Michael."

"I'll call you Nathan," he said.

"What else would you call me?"

"I don't know," Michael said. "Nate?"

"Don't call me Nate. I hate that. I'll be there in thirty minutes. Don't be late."

Michael had to shower too, so he jumped in quick because he wasn't sure how long it'd take to walk to the bus stop at the end of the road. He got dressed without thinking of what to wear and was out the door.

He kept an eye on his phone while he walked to see how long it would take to get to the end of the road. It was hard to tell. There was nothing to look at but gravel, trees, and cornfields. The end of the road didn't feel like it was getting any closer because of the sameness of everything; it looked close and far at once. He was trying to think how long it took to drive it when he was in the car with Pence. It could've been closer to five minutes so walking might be triple that.

He walked faster than he normally would, making him sweat. He kept wiping his brow and tugging at the bottom of his shirt to fan his body and cool himself down. If he went any slower he'd end up leaving Nathan waiting.

When he got to the end of the road, there was a white Nissan sitting at the bus stop. Nathan reached over and popped the door open a bit.

"You look like your photo," he said when Michael got in, studying his face. "That's a good thing."

"Okay," Michael said.

"Why do you live out here? You don't have a car?"

"No. I just moved here."

"Why?"

"I'm not going to be here forever. Just until the end of the semester."

"Yeah, but why?"

"I'll tell you another time."

"It's a good thing you know someone with a car," he said, putting his hand on Michael's thigh. Michael wasn't expecting that, but he didn't mind. He'd never been touched by someone who was this handsome. "Where do you get your groceries?" Nathan asked.

"I don't know," he said. "I just moved here."

"Right. I know a place."

Nathan took him to a No Frills that was a five-minute drive from there. He didn't say anything while he drove, Michael didn't say anything either, but when Nathan parked the car, he took his seatbelt off and turned right around. "You want to kiss me, don't you?"

"Here?" Michael asked. The parking lot was full of cars.

"You don't want to kiss me?"

"I do."

"I'm making you blush," he said. "I like it when you blush. How old are you?"

"Almost nineteen."

"Then kiss me, almost nineteen."

Michael leaned in, put his hand on Nathan's chest, and kissed him even though he imagined that everybody was watching them. His hands were shaking; it was like he had the chills, but Nathan was a good kisser. His lips were warm and he kissed slow, like how people kiss in the movies. The whole thing—people watching, the feeling of Nathan's chest and how he was kissing—it made Michael dizzy. He knew he didn't have to worry about doing stuff like this out in the open. It wasn't a big deal anymore. Nathan didn't worry about it, and he knew he didn't have to either, but it still made him feel dizzy.

Nathan pulled his head back. "How'd you learn to kiss like that?"

"What do you mean?"

"How did you learn to kiss like that? You speak English, don't you?"

"I do."

"I thought you did."

"I don't know how," Michael said.

"You don't know?"

"No."

"A natural, I guess. By the way, you didn't tell me if I looked like my photos too."

"What do you mean?"

"The photos I sent you. Do I look like them?"

"Yes."

"You like how I look?"

"Yeah."

"Good. Do you have a boyfriend?"

"No. Do you?"

"I wouldn't be here if I had a boyfriend. Some guys act like they don't when they do. I don't like that."

"I don't have a boyfriend."

"I'm not saying we're boyfriends. I just want to know the truth."

"It's the truth."

"Good. I don't either. Now let's go shopping."

When they went into the store, Nathan grabbed a shopping cart for Michael and pushed it toward the produce section. "What do you need, anyway?"

Michael felt like people were watching them in there too. Maybe some saw them kissing in the parking lot. He also thought it was weird, two guys shopping together like that. He didn't know what to do with himself, following Nathan around without a shopping cart of his own. Maybe that's why they were staring. He didn't want to care either way, but he cared—that's all he could think of, how people were looking at them because in his head two guys never go shopping together like that unless they're gay.

Nathan stopped pushing the cart. "Do you even know what you need?"

"Pasta."

"Just pasta?"

"No. Coffee too. Maybe some chicken. I should get some chicken and stuff to make salads."

"Did you make a list?"

"No."

"Next time make a list. Promise you will?"

"Okay."

"It'll save us both time."

While they went through the store up and down each aisle, Nathan asked lots of questions: where Michael was from, whether he had siblings, what he was studying, if he liked what he was studying, what he wanted to do after school—there was no end to his questions. Michael asked the exact same questions back after he answered because he was too nervous to think up his own. He was still a hundred percent sure everybody was staring at them and thinking up his own questions was too much for him with that happening too.

He kept an eye out every time they turned a corner, afraid he'd run into someone he knew. Nathan didn't stop with the questions though and didn't mind answering them when Michael asked them back.

At the checkout, Nathan tried to pay but Michael wouldn't let him. At least not at first. Nathan said that he was doing a co-op at a tech start-up, that he was making lots of money, and reminded Michael that he already had a job lined up in Toronto after, so he was doing fine. He said that when he graduated he was going to make lots more so Michael should just let him pay, which he did.

The only thing that bothered Michael about it was the way the cashier was looking him up and down while Nathan was entering his pin into the machine. She didn't stop staring and even gave Michael the receipt once the card went through. He thought Nathan was going to say something about it, how she gave Michael the receipt, but he didn't seem to notice.

"Is your roommate still home?" Nathan asked, before turning the car on.

"Yeah, he is. I should get back."

"What's the address?"

"You can drop me off at the bus stop again."

"Why?"

"I don't mind walking a bit."

"You have too many bags to walk."

"It's fine."

"What, do you live in a crack house? You don't want me to see it?"

"No," Michael said, laughing.

"Then what's the address."

"Serious, I can just walk from the bus stop."

"You think I'm going to stalk you or something? I don't stalk people."

"I don't think that." He looked at the clock in the car. It was only one. Pence wouldn't be back anyway, and Nathan wasn't going to let up, so he told him the address. "You can't come in though," he said. "Maybe another time."

"Another time is fine," he said.

When they pulled into the driveway, Michael worried Pence would be home even though it was too early. He didn't want Nathan to see him since Pence was so much older and looked so gay.

"Is it just you two living here?" Nathan said. "It's a big house for two people."

"I rent out the basement."

"Is it a separate apartment?"

"You have to go through the house."

"You can't have people over?"

"I can. I just moved there though. Yesterday."

"Okay," he said, shrugging like he didn't get it. He popped the trunk open. "Do you want to see me again?"

"Yeah."

"Good." Nathan kissed him with his tongue this time but he did it quick. "I like you."

"I like you too."

"You always repeat what I say."

Michael blushed. "No, I don't."

Nathan kissed him again then unlocked the car doors. "Don't forget to call me later."

Michael brought the groceries into the house and took them to the kitchen. He started laughing hard; he couldn't stop. He thought it was funny meeting Nathan like that, going shopping with someone he didn't know. He didn't think a date could be

43

like that, going shopping and having groceries bought for him. He kept laughing thinking about it, not because he was making fun of Nathan. He liked him and he was handsome. He was nice too, to have paid for the groceries like that. He was laughing because he had a good time and because he never thought he'd do something like that. Especially kissing another guy in a parking lot with other people around. He pretended that it wasn't as scary as it was and he wanted to do it again.

2

Michael lay in bed texting Nathan while he waited for Pence to go to work. He was listening to him upstairs slamming kitchen drawers and whistling loud enough for him to hear from the basement. Michael had the lights off and stayed under the covers in case Pence came down to see if he was sleeping. He wasn't hungry. He could wait another half-hour for breakfast. It had to be a half-hour if Pence was going to make it to work in time.

His phone lit the basement when a new message came in from Nathan. He was trying to get Michael to go to the university later even if he wasn't going to class. He said he wanted to see him; he missed him and he never missed anybody.

Michael wasn't up for it, but said he'd only go if Nathan picked him up.

I will but I'm not going to the bus stop again, Nathan wrote.

You promise not to stalk me if I tell you my address?

Bitch LOL. I know your address.

Are you stalking me?

I'll be there at 10.

Michael waited a couple minutes after Pence left to go upstairs in case he'd forgotten something and came back. He didn't feel like talking. Pence kept bringing up what had happened with his mom and how he was feeling about it. He made it out like it was better to talk about it than not, even though Michael didn't feel that way. They say stuff like that on TV too—that it's better to talk than not—but just because they say it doesn't mean it works for everyone. Michael was feeling fine without having to talk about it every second.

○

After he showered he put paste in his hair. He never did that, but he thought it'd be nice. He used some he found in Pence's bathroom. It didn't look cheap. It was in a clay jar that was hard to open. It smelled like earth.

He did his hair in a way he'd never done before, pushing the back part down and front up. Nathan looked good and he wanted to look good too.

When Nathan came he smelled like aftershave. It was a minty, peppery smell. Nathan said that Michael smelled nice too and reached across the car console to kiss him. He thought how nice it was to have someone to kiss like that. He liked how they took their time doing it, letting their lips play together.

Nathan grabbed on to Michael's thigh again while he was driving. He did it the whole way to school and would sometimes rub it and squeeze it. When they'd stop at a traffic light he'd look over and wink. Michael would smile back.

"Are you going to introduce me to your friends?" Nathan said when they got to school.

"I haven't made a lot of friends here."

"Aren't you from Kitchener?"

"Yeah."

"I thought lots of people would've come here for school."

"Some people but not my friends."

"Well, you're going to meet my friends," he said. "I know lots of people."

"Nice people?"

"My friends will be your friends."

He followed Nathan through the student centre to the cafeteria. It was the exact same as it always was. Everything for him had changed since he was there last, but school stayed the same. People sat and studied how they always did; they drank their coffees or played on their phones. It was going to keep going with or without him. It'd be like this tomorrow too and the day after, even if he died. Nobody would do anything differently. If he were buried in the ground next week, nobody would care except Nathan maybe. He'd probably be the only one even though he hardly knew him. He'd probably be surprised if he died. It wouldn't last long though. He'd remember him less each day like it didn't matter. And it didn't matter. Nobody mattered. If any of the people in the cafeteria died, it'd be the same. People might remember them longer than they'd remember Michael, but they'd probabaly forget them too. And if they didn't, the people that remembered would die, so who cares?

Michael just wanted to feel good. That's what mattered. He wanted to feel good and be happy. While he walked next to Nathan, he thought to reach out for his hand. He knew he could. Nathan wouldn't stop him. When their hands swung by each other he was about to. Their fingers touched. He knew people would stare: people who knew him, or knew him to see him. Nobody did stuff like that at school unless they looked like it—if they had hair dyed bright colours or piercings on their face. They were the only ones who didn't care.

Their hands swung by each other again. Michael was about to grab on. He reached out but missed. Maybe Nathan wouldn't want to. He believed he would, but what if he didn't and thought it was weird to do it in front of everyone? Michael didn't have it in him to try again. Instead, he put his hand on Nathan's back and gave it a quick rub. Nathan turned to him and smiled. Michael thought he was going to kiss him like he did at No Frills but he didn't. He smiled but kept walking.

Nathan's friends were at the other end of the cafeteria. There was a big group of them sitting around two tables. They were all handsome like Nathan. Girls, guys: all of them were good-looking and had on clothes that looked brand new and clean haircuts.

Nathan went to the end of the table and gave a long wave. Some waved back and some just said hi. The guy closest to him started talking about an exam that was coming up. Michael was pretending to listen but felt nervous standing there. Nathan didn't say anything about him to his friends. Some of them were staring—they seemed confused—but they didn't say anything.

The guy Nathan was talking to acted like Michael wasn't there. He was naming things he thought would be on the exam. Nathan was saying whether he thought he was right or wrong. His friend agreed with whatever he was saying even if it was the opposite of what he'd said.

The way Nathan was talking made his face change. It got serious in a way Michael didn't like. He wouldn't have recognized him if he was walking by. It's probably why he never noticed him before. They'd talked about that: how they were at the cafeteria every day but they never saw each other. That's probably why. He looked different when he was talking like that.

"I'm going to go to class," Michael said. He felt he needed to leave.

Nathan's friend looked over at him. It was like he was seeing him for the first time. He smiled but didn't say anything.

Nathan's face went back to normal. It was different and now it wasn't, but it didn't help. Michael needed to get out of there.

"You're going already?" Nathan grinned but his face turned red.

"I have to go to class."

"Are you sure?" He was confused now.

"Yeah. If I'm here I should go."

"Are you going to meet me after?"

"I'll text when I'm done."

It looked like Nathan wanted to say something else. His face was trying to; it looked like he was worried but he patted Michael on the back and made him promise to text.

o

Michael left the student centre and walked from one end of the campus to the other along paved paths and through the grassy lawns between the lecture halls and other buildings. The sun was out and it felt like summer was coming even though there was supposed to be snow later in the week. The sun felt good; he didn't want to think about the snow or that the worst of winter was coming.

When he got to the other end of the campus near University Avenue, he could see the coffee shop where he'd first met Pence. It got him thinking about how different life would've been if he hadn't gone there to meet him. He wasn't sure if it'd be good or bad, but it'd be different if he'd never talked to him online or swapped pictures.

He kept walking to the coffee shop for a drink. He hadn't been since his meeting with Pence, and he wanted to see it again. He didn't know if he liked the feeling of being back.

Walking over, his stomach felt funny the way it did the last time. It reminded him of what it was like when he had a crush on Pence.

He opened the door; the smell of the coffee shop was sweet. He remembered that. It wasn't like other coffee shops. He figured it was from the different hot chocolates they made. They had four flavours. It brought him right back to that day.

He got a medium coffee and went to the spot they'd sat at that day. It was by the window. He sat in the exact same seat and remembered Pence in the other one. It made him like Pence more, being back. He figured life wasn't that bad.

He sat back with his arms crossed. It was good sitting there, thinking that this was the way things needed to be. Life would've been different if he hadn't come here with Pence. It would've been different if he didn't tell his mom he was gay too, but he had to do these things; he couldn't not do them.

He took his time drinking his coffee. He thought about Pence, meeting him that day, and watched people pass by the window. He took the coffee lid off and had sips that were barely sips. He wasn't in a hurry for anything. He didn't give Nathan a time to meet so he was relaxed.

He didn't know how long he was sitting there. His mind went somewhere else. Michael finished his coffee before realizing it. He picked up the paper coffee cup like it still had coffee in it. He held it up and stared at more people passing by. He tried to take a sip, but it was all gone. He shook it a bit and put it back down.

○

He walked back to the student centre across the campus. Classes must've gotten out at once because the lawns between the lecture halls filled with people.

He decided he wasn't going to text Nathan unless he texted him first. He didn't like how his face changed and figured if it was meant to be, it was meant to be.

He checked his phone every few seconds in case he texted. He hadn't, so Michael took it as a sign.

The student centre was as full as the lawn areas. There were lines forming through the crowds, going to the cafeteria or the back of the building where the buses came. Michael had to stop and sidestep to get through.

He watched for Nathan, thinking that if he saw him, he'd go talk to him. It'd be a sign, so he kept an eye out. It was so busy he had to stop walking altogether a couple of times and wait for people to move. He did a quick spin around to make sure Nathan wasn't there but was able to move from the front to the back of the building without seeing him.

There was a long driveway on the other side where the buses came. Michael got his phone out to figure out how to get to Pence's on the bus. He'd never tried and needed to know. He'd be doing it every day next week. He was hoping there'd be a direct bus. He hated transferring.

While he was figuring it out, a Greyhound came up the drive and stopped right in front of him. Before he figured out how to get to Pence's, it was there in front of him.

The driver got off and shouted, "Toronto!"

He didn't have a ticket but told himself that if Nathan didn't text by the time everyone got on, he'd get on too. He took this as a sign too. He hadn't been to Toronto in a while; he had nothing to do, so why not go?

It took a couple of minutes for everyone to board the bus. The driver was organizing the luggage on the sidewalk before piling it into the side compartment. He had a cigarette after that. Michael got on just as he finished.

He thought Nathan might message him on the way to Toronto, but he didn't. He kept checking every twenty minutes on the drive over.

o

It took longer to get to Toronto than it usually did. There was lots of traffic, and it made a stop in Mississauga at Square One mall. That added an extra thirty minutes to the drive. It was close to six by the time it pulled into the Toronto station.

When he got off the bus, he was feeling hungry, so he found a place to get a pizza slice and walked around the Eaton Centre while he ate it. When he finished, he left the mall and went to the liquor store in the Atrium on Bay. He picked up two mickeys of vodka and took them to the public washroom down from the shop. He emptied out the water bottle that he had in his school bag and filled it up with one of the mickeys. There was no one in the bathroom so he did it out in the open and took a big gulp before shutting it. It made him want to throw up—he didn't like the taste, but it made him feel good inside a few seconds later.

He left the Atrium and wandered up Yonge Street through the crowds. It was starting to get dark and the store signs were lighting the street. There were cars driving by, playing songs with heavy bass, someone was shouting verses from the bible over a megaphone, breakdancers were beatboxing and kicking their legs around, and these two guys were playing the drums on overturned buckets.

Michael took another sip of his bottle, and it wasn't as bad the second time. If he didn't let it touch his tongue too much, it was fine.

He stopped at the door of Denim, a Yonge Street bar that had blackened windows and a pride flag hanging up top. It was the spot where he usually turned off Yonge to head to the gay village on Church Street. The flag let him know it was time to turn.

He took another sip and thought about going in. He'd gone to places on Church but never here. It was on a busy part of Yonge, and he worried about straight people seeing him go in. It was easy on Church, everyone was the same. But he always wondered about this place.

He took another sip and tugged at the door. It was stuck, so he pulled harder to get it open. He stepped into a long hall. It was so dark it was hard to see where he was walking. The bottoms of his shoes were sticking to the floor and there was the smell of stale beer and cigarettes, like they let people smoke in there.

At the end of the hall was a small room full of people and a bar in the middle of it. The only light was coming from the beer fridges and the two slot machines set up on either side of the bar. When his eyes adjusted to the darkness, he noticed that everyone was either really young or old. There was nothing in between. The young ones were his age but rough looking: lots of them had sunken eyes and cheekbones like blades. They didn't seem to mind being passed around by the older ones, who were two to three times their size. They had big hands to grope them, and the young men would get caught between their bellies. Michael didn't get what was going on here; he'd never seen anything like it on Church Street.

His mouth was wide open when he got to the bar, the server said he was going to catch a fly if he didn't shut it. The bartender had a curly moustache and a ball cap on backwards. Before Michael could say anything, the guy next to him with rotten teeth and a trucker hat said he wanted to buy him a drink. His breath smelled like rotten fish and came from deep in his bowels.

"I need to go to the bathroom," Michael said to the bartender.

He'd annoyed the bartender somehow. "Then go to the bathroom."

"Where is it?"

That annoyed him more, but he pointed to a staircase that wasn't far from where they were standing. Michael went in that direction but kept his eyes on the ground. He went to the basement, locked himself in a stall and took three sips from the water bottle, finishing most of the vodka. He filled it with the other mickey in his bag and thought that he had to get out of there. The people were off. He'd always wondered what it was like, and now he knew. He was happy he went but wanted out.

He took another sip—a bigger one this time—and wiped his mouth with his sleeve.

He went upstairs and walked back through the bar past the bartender, who was saying something to him. He ignored it and ignored the guy with the rotten teeth, who was also saying something.

He was about to push the front door to get out, but it opened before he could. He stumbled, but the guy who'd opened it grabbed his arm and lifted him so he wouldn't fall. He was older and stocky but looked like an actor from TV because of how tan he was.

"Are you okay?" he said.

"I'm fine."

"Are you leaving?"

"I guess."

"But I just got here."

Michael looked over his shoulder to make sure the guy was talking to him. It was just the two of them, though, but he didn't get it. The guy was talking like he knew him. Or maybe he was mistaking him for someone else. "I don't know," Michael said.

He laughed. "What don't you know?"

Michael shrugged.

"So, you're going to run out on me like this?"

"I don't know," Michael said again.

"You keep saying that."

Silence.

"What if I get lonely by myself?"

They were starting to get the attention of the people on the street. Some were staring at them in the doorway. He didn't want the attention—he didn't get what was happening, and he needed to get out of there so they'd stop looking.

He shrugged again and moved away from the door and kept walking. He didn't stop.

"I didn't mean to scare you," the guy said. It seemed like he meant it, but Michael kept going up Yonge and turned onto Isabella Street. He didn't know what else to do; he didn't like how people were looking.

The farther he got, the more he got thinking, and when he got to Church Street it hit him. The guy was flirting with him. That's why he was talking like that. It was dumb Michael didn't see it. Michael stopped walking and thought about going back. He didn't get that the guy was flirting when it was happening, but it made him smile to think that that's what it was. He thought the guy looked good; he was clean; he wasn't like the other ones there. If he knew he was flirting, he would've talked some more, but what was he going to say now? If he went back he'd have nothing to say. What happened happened, and now it passed. He couldn't think of what to say if he went back. He didn't want to look dumb by having nothing to say.

He turned around again and kept going to Church Street. He couldn't go back if he had nothing to say.

He went to Woody's on Church Street because he knew it'd be the busiest bar and he wasn't wrong. It was hard to walk inside because there were so many people, but he'd rather it be busy than not.

He pushed his way through, trying to find where the bathroom was. He had to ask around and was told it was in the basement.

He took a piss, then had more vodka right at the urinal. He didn't care about the other people there. He was drinking from a water bottle anyway. It just looked like he was drinking water. After he washed his hands, he had more, but then things got blurry, more than he would've liked. It had happened before he realized it. He moved out of the bathroom, up the steps. He went through the crowd, but he didn't know where he was going. He was just moving. There was lots of music and talking. There was laughing, making him feel like he was spinning around. He needed somewhere to sit. He didn't need another drink. He needed a seat to relax.

The bar seemed to go forever. He couldn't see the walls because of all the people. The bass from the music was making people move. Michael kept bumping into guys and pushing them out of the way.

He found an empty stool by a pillar. Trying to sit made him spin more but once he got on the seat, it was better. He didn't need another drink. He needed to not move. He thought closing his eyes would help, but it made things spin again. He opened them and grabbed on tight to the two sides of the stool and didn't move for thirty minutes. He was trying to feel normal again. He got it in his head that the guy from Denim was coming, so he had to be normal. He wasn't going to ruin it again.

After an hour, he was starting to feel better. Nothing was spinning anymore. He still had some vodka left, but he didn't need any of that. He got a beer and drank it slowly. He didn't want to spin again but didn't want to lose the buzz. If the guy came, he wanted to have a personality so he kept drinking, but beer was better than vodka because it was hard to drink it fast.

Another hour passed, and the place started emptying out. He could start seeing the walls because there weren't a lot of people there. It felt smaller. He could walk across the place in a few seconds. It would've taken ten minutes before, but when he went to get another drink it was easy.

Even when it got to closing time, Michael told himself he was going to see the Denim guy. Maybe not at the bar, but the night wasn't over. It could be on the street, somewhere else; he was going to see him. He finished his beer and got up. He wasn't sober but he wasn't spinning. He was drunk but wasn't going to fall over. He could walk straight like it was nothing.

The bars all closed at once and the streets were filled with people. There were lines for burgers, pizza and poutine. People were shouting and saying stupid things, and their friends were laughing at those stupid things. Everyone was drunk like Michael. He wasn't shouting like them, but he wasn't alone. He walked up the side of the road. He was between the moving cars and the parked ones, keeping an eye out for the Denim guy. He walked slowly, but he was feeling good. Even if the Denim guy didn't show, he was having fun. He couldn't have a night like this in Waterloo.

He stopped at a pizza shop at Church and Wellesley. There wasn't a line like at the other shops. He went in, grabbed a slice, and was back on the road, walking by parked cars. There was someone walking on the road too, about twenty feet ahead of him. He started following him without thinking. He could see him there, but he wasn't really looking. He was eating his slice.

The guy stopped at a red light and grabbed a cigarette from his pocket. Michael stopped too; it's when he really noticed him. He was a few feet away.

Michael kept following him when the light turned green. He couldn't see his face, but he started wondering if it was the guy from Denim. He had the same shoulders. He was shorter but with wide shoulders. His hair was brown on the sides but had grey on the top. When Michael noticed all this, he was sure it was him. Pretty sure, but it was hard to know without seeing his face. He didn't remember the grey hair, but it doesn't mean it wasn't grey. Everything else looked the same. It was just the hair he wasn't sure about, and his face.

He moved his legs faster, trying to catch up so he could get a better look. If it was him, he'd talk to him properly. He didn't know what he was going to say, except he was going to say something—it didn't matter what it was. He figured if he just said something, anything, it'd get things going. He'd had enough to drink, he wasn't scared.

He dragged his heels, hoping the guy could hear him coming. There was no way he couldn't hear with the noise he was making. Michael was about to pass. They got shoulder to shoulder, but the guy stopped walking. Michael thought it was because of him. He figured he was going to say something, that Michael wouldn't have to say something first. Michael stopped too. He was waiting for it. The guy turned the other way though. He didn't notice him there. It was like Michael was invisible. How didn't he hear him?

The guy took a last drag from his cigarette and threw it and went up some stairs into a red low-rise building.

Michael thought it was where he lived, but there was a sign next to the stairs. It was a sauna called Fluid. It was just for men. Michael had never been to a bathhouse before. He knew what they were. He'd read about them—no street clothes allowed, you have to wear a towel—that's what he knew, and that they were for sex. There were a few in the city, but he never thought to go. He wouldn't know what to do, but he wasn't going to let the guy get away, so he went up the stairs.

There was a guy in a glass booth on the other side of the door who was on his phone. When he noticed Michael, he said, "You can't bring food in here."

Michael forgot he had pizza in his hand. It was half eaten, folded up.

"You'll have to go outside to eat it."

"Sorry," Michael said.

"You just can't bring it in here."

"Okay."

He went back out and tried to eat it quickly, as he started doubting that it was the Denim guy in there. He didn't want to go back if it wasn't, but he wouldn't know unless he did. He finished the slice and washed it down with vodka. He wished he had water for it. The vodka didn't go with the pizza, but it made him feel calm about having to go back in.

"Can I help you?" The guy behind the booth didn't acknowledge that he'd just been there. Michael could tell by his face. He was looking right through him.

Michael asked for a room, but all were taken except one on the first floor. The guy said it was expensive because it had a sling in it. He said it was popular and would be gone soon if he didn't take it. Michael didn't know what a sling was—he thought it was something like a slingshot—but said he'd take the room anyway.

He got a key and a towel and the door next to him buzzed. He looked at the door; he didn't get what the buzzing was for.

"Go in," the guy said.

"Go in?"

"Pull the door."

Michael pulled and went into a dark hall. It had small lockers piled on top of each other. They went all the way down on both sides. Blue lights were coming from under them. It was the only light. It made it look like he was underwater: his skin was blue, his clothes and the lockers—it was all blue.

There was a spicy smell from the saunas. There was the smell of sweat and shit too. It was like the locker room at the Y. There was lots to smell.

Michael went through the halls and heard lockers slamming. There were guys in towels hiding in the shadows where the blue lights didn't go. He couldn't see faces because of how the lights were. He could just see body shapes. He didn't know how he'd recognize the Denim guy if he could only see his body and not his face. He didn't know him from his body.

His key tag had 114 written on it. The hall with the rooms started at 164.

Some doors were open. He'd look in and see some guys who were pulling at their dicks. It was that, or they had their asses up to get fucked. Their doors were wide open. They didn't care who looked in.

Michael found his room at the end of the first floor, in a corner. He went in and turned the light on full. There was a leather thing hanging from the ceiling. It was like a hammock but there were metal loops all over it. A bed was up against the wall with no pillow and a locker next to it.

If he sat on the bed, he would've passed out. Even without a pillow, it would've been easy. He had to focus—he didn't come to sleep. He whacked his face with both hands to wake himself and then took his clothes and shoes off. He put them in the locker and had more vodka.

He wrapped the towel around himself and went back to the hall. It felt like they'd turned the music up. It was making him dizzy: either the music or the vodka. He had to keep his head up to see who was coming. He was trying to keep his eyes open for the Denim guy. He could make out faces but only when they were close up. He'd have to squint sometimes.

He felt he was walking in circles. Parts of the sauna were lit blue but some were black. He reached his hand out in the darker parts to find his way. If he got too close to people, they'd reach out. Some would grab him. He couldn't see their faces in the dark. They'd grab an arm or leg, and one even reached under his towel and tried to grab his dick. Michael said no thank you. He tried to stop him but he wouldn't stop; he got tangled up in him so he had to whack him away. "Fuck off," Michael said. That was the last thing he remembered before he passed out.

o

Michael woke up in his room with the sling. He didn't know where he was right away. His mouth was dry. It felt like his throat was going to close up. That, and his brain was scrambled. When he lifted his head, it felt worse. It was like he got smacked in the face with a frying pan.

It took him a second to figure out he wasn't in Pence's basement because the lights in the room were down low. He sat up quickly and made sure he was alone. His towel was on the floor; his jeans and shirt were back on. The door was closed, he was by himself but he couldn't remember getting dressed or how he got to his room.

He rubbed at his eyes; it helped with his head. When he stood up, he got dizzy again but he needed to get out of there. He went back out into the hall. There was nobody there anymore. House music was coming from the speakers but it was quiet. The place was empty, not how he remembered it.

He found his way out of the sauna, but when he got to the street he had to squint because of the sun, and his eyes watered.

His throat was still dry; it was hard to swallow. He needed something to drink. He thought it'd help with his head too so he stopped at a store, down from the sauna. He got a one-litre bottle of water and chugged it at the store counter after he paid. It helped, but now his stomach hurt so he went to McDonald's and got two egg sandwiches with extra cheese and an extra-large coffee. He sat in a booth and switched his phone on. He wanted to check the bus timetables, but a pile of messages came in from Nathan and Pence. His phone kept buzzing, but he didn't feel like reading them. He told himself he'd take a look on the bus back home. He fell asleep once he got on the bus though and didn't wake up until he got back to Waterloo.

The bus dropped him off at the school again. There weren't many people there. It was Saturday and quiet. Even in the student centre, there was hardly anyone.

He got another coffee from the cafeteria and took a seat by the window. He didn't know how to take the bus back to Pence's. He'd have to look it up too, but he didn't feel like it right away. He still had a headache and wanted to take it easy. He took the lid off his coffee and blew on the top. There was no reason to rush.

He hadn't thought about the Denim guy all morning. He almost forgot it was why he went to Fluid. He still didn't know if it was him there yesterday. It could've been. There was no way of knowing, but he thought how he was going to find him. He'd go back to Toronto next week; he'd go to Denim again. Even if he had to stay all weekend, he was going to find him.

He was forgetting what he looked like. He could see his blue eyes and how he smiled. He was tanned—he remembered that. He'd know him to see him.

o

When Michael got back, Pence was on the sofa reading a paper.

"Well, it's nice of you to join us today," he said.

Michael thought it was a joke.

"Where've you been?" Pence said.

"At a friend's. We were having drinks."

"This morning?"

He laughed. "No, yesterday." Silence. "I passed out on his couch."

"I thought you were dead in a ditch."

He laughed again. Was it a joke? "I just drank too much."

"You didn't think to text when you woke up?"

"I saw your messages, but I had a headache."

Pence looked back down at the newspaper. He turned the page. "Which friend were you having drinks with?"

"Sky," he said. It was the first name he thought of.

"Sky?"

"Yeah."

"What kind of name is that?"

"What do you mean?" There was a guy in class named Sky—he wasn't making it up, but they weren't friends.

"Are they from here?"

"They're from school."

"From Canada?"

"I don't know. Maybe Korea."

"Well, I know it wasn't Nate."

"Who?"

"Nate. He came by here looking for you last night."

Silence.

"I don't know what you're talking about," Michael said.

"Nate." He looked up from the paper.

"Nathan?"

"I would think so. I thought he was your boyfriend but obviously not." Pence let out a loud "Ha!"

"We just met."

"You're all over the place, aren't you? Why don't you get some sleep?"

"Thanks." He went for the basement door.

"Are you going to be out all night again tonight or will you be home for dinner?"

"I'm not going out."

"Be ready at seven then. I'm making dinner. We need to talk."

"Okay. Sounds nice."

"This isn't a flophouse," Pence said. "Pull yourself together. You look like shit."

o

Michael went to bed and stayed in bed for the rest of the day. Nathan tried to text some more so Michael let him know he was okay. He said something came up. Nathan tried calling once he'd sent the text but he didn't feel like talking. He turned his phone off.

He went back upstairs late that afternoon. Pence was in the kitchen cooking. Michael told him that it smelled good. He was trying to make things better before going up to shower because he could tell Pence was still mad.

"I appreciate that," Pence said. "You better be hungry."

He made blackened chicken, scalloped potatoes, and cornbread. Michael had heard of cornbread but never tried it. He didn't think he'd liked it by the name, but it was sweeter than he thought it'd be. It tasted like cake.

Everything else was good too—he kept telling Pence that because it seemed to make him happy to hear it, and he wanted to keep him happy. If he was happy then he wouldn't be on his case. He wasn't lying either, though. It was good; he hadn't eaten properly all day.

The wine made the night easier. When they got to the second bottle, Michael started having fun. He didn't have to pretend. Pence was having fun too but wasn't drinking as much. He was leaning back in his chair with his hands behind his head. He wasn't saying anything; he was listening to Michael talk about being back at school yesterday. Michael also told him how he stopped at the coffee shop that they'd met at. He said how he hadn't been there since they'd met. Pence liked that and asked why he went but Michael couldn't say why. He just started walking and ended up there.

When they got to the third bottle of wine, Pence asked who Nathan was. Michael said it wasn't serious; it's how he answered the question and he laughed when he told him about going to No Frills together.

Pence said he was good-looking, probably trying to get more out of him. Michael agreed but said they were still getting to know each other. Pence asked if they were fucking, and Michael said they weren't because they weren't. Pence didn't believe it. "You can tell me," he said. "Come on. You can tell me. It's not a big deal."

It was the truth. He told him how Nathan picked him up yesterday to take him to school. It was just that and No Frills. They'd just met.

"You fucked." Pence sat up and crossed his arms over the table. "I don't know why you're not telling me."

"We didn't," Michael laughed. "I swear."

"You think I'd be mad?"

"I'd say if we did."

"Okay, you didn't," he said. He pushed the plate away. Michael didn't know what to do, so he started collecting the dishes.

"Do you plan on staying in the basement long-term?" Pence said.

Michael had to think about it. Then he said, "If you don't mind. Until I figure things out."

"Put those down. The dishes. Put them down. We need to talk."

Michael sat down again.

"I don't mind you staying. I don't." He smiled and started picking at his nails. "The thing is," Pence said, but stopped again. "The thing is, I think it's only fair that you start paying your way."

Michael would have trouble paying rent since he was working part-time. He took a couple of shifts at the grocery store each week, but he said that he'd drop a class to work more if he needed to. He probably had to drop a class anyway; he needed to make money. "It'll take longer to finish school, but I don't mind."

"You don't need to do that," Pence said.

"I can't afford to pay rent. I'm going to have to do it anyway."

"I miss being with you."

It wasn't what Michael thought he was going to say. He was quiet because it wasn't what he was expecting. He looked down at himself and said, "I'm right here."

"Silly boy. I miss *being* with you. Having you in my bed."

"We're just friends. We talked about this already."

Pence smiled.

"We agreed," Michael said.

"We didn't agree. You decided."

"I love you as a friend, but not like that. We're like family."

Pence laughed. He grabbed his wine and slurped some. "Sex doesn't have to be about love," he said. "Look at me. Do you hear me? It's not about love. Maybe just once a week we have some fun." He shrugged. "You need experience anyway. I can teach you things, and you won't need to worry about rent or food. I'll take care of all that. You focus on school. You need to finish school. We can't have you dropping classes. Do you understand?"

This was never part of the deal. Pence had said that he could stay for as long as he needed. There was never anything in there about this.

"Will *Nate* take you in?" Pence said.

"Who?" Michael sounded more bothered than he could afford to be.

"Your new lover."

Michael calmed himself down. "I don't have a lover," he said, trying to be as normal as he could be.

"Relax. Don't get mad. Look, if you want to stay, you can keep your bedroom downstairs. No problem. But you have to pay your way."

Michael closed his eyes.

"Am I that bad?" Pence said.

Michael kept his eyes shut for as long as he could without it ruining things. He knew if he ruined things it'd be bad. It'd be even worse than this.

He opened his eyes. Pence was smiling. It was a friendly smile, but he was sad too, like he felt bad for him.

"You're not bad," Michael said. "I'm just tired from last night."

Pence chuckled. "That's not very convincing."

"No. You're helping me."

"I am. I care. I always will. I'm going to keep helping you." He came around to Michael. "Give me a hug. Stand up." Michael did as he was told. He squeezed Pence and tried to mean it. He acted like he didn't mind when Pence put his face between his shoulder and neck.

"It's going to be okay. I promise. I'll take care of you. Your life is in my hands. Remember?" Pence pulled his head back. He looked Michael in the eye. "Remember?"

"I remember."

"I've missed you," he said. "I hate being like this. It's just that I've missed us."

He started kissing Michael and Michael let him. He let him do whatever he wanted. It was the easiest thing, and it wasn't as bad as he thought it'd be.

o

After midnight, Michael went into the kitchen and poured some more wine. He filled his glass all the way to the top and drank half of it all at once. He poured more and took the glass out to the yard.

It was so dark out. He couldn't see anything. He turned his phone light on, but it was still too dark to see.

He started walking on the grass to the forest in the back. He wanted to see the trees, as if it'd make things better. He kept going until he got to them and shined the light up into the branches. It made him smile; he didn't know why. He just needed to see them.

He leaned against one of the tree trunks and looked back at Pence's place. The only light was coming from the kitchen.

It was so quiet he could feel it in his ears.

He remembered the wine. He took a sip and decided to drink slow so he didn't need to go back for more. It felt good in his stomach; he wrapped both hands around the glass. He didn't know good wine from bad wine, but he liked it.

He closed his eyes and tried to remember what the guy from Denim looked like. He could see his eyes. He remembered them. He could see his smile too, but there was a lot of him he couldn't see. He got worried that he'd forget him altogether. He had to work to keep him in his head.

3

Nathan wasn't happy. Michael knew because of texts he'd sent. Michael didn't respond back to them, and that made Nathan send even more where he sounded really pissed. He said there was something wrong with Michael; he meant that he was fucked in the head. But he said he was happy to see his true colours.

He brought up Pence, and asked if they were together. He thought it was disgusting if it was true. Michael didn't write back to that either, so Nathan said it was true. He said it was "fucking disgusting" and he didn't respect anyone who had a sugar daddy.

Michael went back to school the next week but didn't go to the student centre. He didn't want to run into Nathan. He'd probably say even worse things if he saw him. If he was getting texts like that, it'd be bad. He knew why he was mad—he'd probably be mad too if things were the other way around—but he had to focus. He couldn't be thinking about this stuff. He needed to get caught up at school.

During some classes, Michael was able to take his mind off things. He'd write down everything his professors were saying. Even if it wasn't important, he'd write it down. He took pages of notes because it cleared his head. He could only think about what he was writing down.

By Friday he was all caught up. The week had gone by without him noticing. He had two shifts at the grocery store: Tuesday and Thursday. If he wasn't working, he was studying and it was starting to feel like how things used to be.

He got a bus ticket to Toronto for Friday after class. He didn't go through the student centre to get to the bus pick-up either. He walked around it because he knew he might run into Nathan if he went through.

Even though he didn't want to see him, when the bus got going, he started writing a text message to him. His head was leaning against the window, and he was typing slowly but kept adding things and deleting things. He was trying to figure out what to say. He wasn't planning to text him since he'd been avoiding him but he just started doing it. After ten minutes of writing and revising, he decided to just write, *I'm sorry*, and pressed Send.

It showed that Nathan read it right away. He thought he'd write something back. The three dots appeared showing that he was writing, but then they went away.

Michael waited twenty minutes. He figured Nathan was thinking of what to say. He knew why Nathan might not say anything, but he wanted him to say something.

When the bus got near Guelph, Nathan still hadn't written anything so Michael figured he wasn't going to. Maybe he didn't believe his apology; Michael felt he had to prove it. He didn't mean to do what he did. It wasn't nice ignoring him. He sent another message, said he was sorry, and that he knew it wasn't nice what he did. Nathan read that right away, but he didn't write back to that either.

Michael lifted his head from the window to help him think. Nathan wasn't going to respond; he needed more than that. Michael knew it so he gave him more. He said how he was kicked out of his parents' house. It's why he wasn't going to class—it'd just happened; he'd needed time off. He figured that telling Nathan this was the only way to get him to write back. He said he had nowhere to go. That's why he was staying with Pence. It was the only place. He told him that Pence was a high school teacher. He wasn't his teacher, but he taught at the school he went to. They were friends. That was it. Pence let him crash in the basement, but Michael wanted his own place in the summer. He said he was sorry again. He said it wasn't nice what he did.

He also told him how he was going to Toronto for the night. *Maybe we can hang out when I get back*, he wrote.

Nathan didn't respond.

○

Michael didn't get to Denim until after seven. He went right from the Greyhound station. It was busy, but he found a seat at the bar.

The bartender with the curly moustache and ball cap was there again. He was standing around, with a rag over his shoulder and was bobbing his head to classic rock coming from the juke-box. He acted like he couldn't see Michael waiting for a drink. Michael had to wave him down to get his attention. The guy waved back in the same way Michael did and came over but took his time, walking slow.

"A Molson," Michael said.

The bartender repeated the order: "A Molson."

He poured the drink and went back to listening to the music.

A lot of the guys there were the same age as Michael but they weren't like him. He'd never let himself be passed around the way they did like it was nothing. He didn't get it: they'd let the older ones do whatever they wanted. They could kiss their necks, put their hands down their pants, rub at their chests—whatever they wanted.

The young ones weren't pretty, but they had youth and that was worth something. Michael didn't know a lot of things, but he knew that. It didn't make sense to give it away for nothing.

"You look lonely," one of the big boys said. He grabbed the stool next to Michael but was having trouble sitting on it properly. That's how big he was, groaning while he tried to find the right spot. He was all fat and muscle but looked like he'd been in good shape once. His arms were big but his gut was bigger. It was round but solid.

When he got in his seat, he lifted his glass. His fist was in Michael's face. "Cheers," he said. His hands were fat and muscular too. They were twice as big as Michael's.

Michael lifted his glass but didn't say anything. He wasn't here for this.

The big boy told him again that he looked lonely. "There's something sad about you," he said. "A lost boy."

"I'm fine," Michael said.

He cleared his throat but it made him cough. Then he grinned: "You *are* fine," he said. "My lost boy."

He had big lips that looked stretched because they were so big. It looked like they could be popped with a pin. He had a big face too, for the big lips. His eyes, though, they were sunk into the head. They were hardly there.

He cleared his throat again—he wasn't smiling anymore. "If someone pays you a compliment you should thank them. Do you hear me, boy, or are you going to keep ignoring me? I said if someone pays you a compliment, you thank them. Didn't your mom teach you manners?"

The bartender was looking right at Michael too. He was waiting for him to say something.

"Okay. Thanks," Michael said.

"You're welcome. Some people are just so ungrateful," he said
to the bartender, but he turned back to Michael. "Why are you
here anyway, boy?"

"He got lost," the bartender said. "A lost boy." He went to
serve someone.

"Are you a lost boy?"

"I didn't get lost."

"Is that right?"

"I've been here before," Michael said.

"Last week he came right in and went right out," the bartender
said in the middle of serving another big boy. "We scared him."

"Did we scare you?"

"Is it against the law, me being here?" Michael said. It surprised
them, what he said. It surprised him too. It wasn't like him to
stand up for himself like that. He wasn't here for this though.

"Is it against the law?" the big boy repeated. He laughed but
that made him start coughing again. He had to clear his throat.
"Bobby, is it against the law?"

"Might be," the bartender said. "If you're not being discreet."

"I got handcuffs at home," he said to Michael. "I'd have fun
with an asshole like you."

He didn't get why they were talking to him. He did nothing
to them. He wanted to leave but couldn't. He didn't come to
Toronto to leave.

"I'm meeting someone," Michael said.

"He's meeting someone," the big boy told the bartender.
"How much is he paying you?"

"I wouldn't pay a cent for this one," the bartender said. "A dud."

"I'll pay you double what he's paying."

The guy must've seen how mad he was making Michael. His
face was all red. Michael didn't know it but it showed. He never

got like that. He didn't like being talked to like he was nothing. He'd been waiting all week to come. He'd worked hard; it was a shit week. It was a shit two weeks. He didn't come for this.

He was mad and didn't know how to hide it. It was so bad the big boy said that he was sorry. He was laughing but he said sorry. He started coughing again but told him to relax. He couldn't laugh without coughing. He cleared his throat. "Let me buy you a drink, boy," he said. "I was just joking with you. I'm a nice guy, I swear. Bobby, tell him."

"He's one of the best guys I know. Seriously."

"I like to fuck around," he said. "Not everyone gets my humour. My parents are British."

"One of the best guys."

"Let me buy you a drink. Whatever you want." He noticed Michael's empty beer glass. "He wants another beer," he told the bartender.

"A Molson," the bartender said. He poured it into a fresh glass.

The big boy wanted to cheers again. He held his glass up and said, "To new friends."

"Thanks," Michael said. They smacked their glasses together. Michael couldn't afford not to accept a free drink.

"I'm Terry."

"I'm Stewart," Michael said.

"See? I'm a nice guy. I'm not just saying that. If you get to know me, you'll get to know my humour."

"One of the funniest guys I know," the bartender said before he went to go serve someone else.

"I don't pay him to say that." His smile was like he was trying to be charming. He was probably handsome years ago. Michael didn't know how old he was, but he knew it was old because of how the skin wrinkled around his collar.

"You're not from here," the guy said.

"No."

"I can tell. Where are you from?"

"Waterloo."

"At the university?"

"Yeah."

"What's a smart boy like you doing in a place like this?"

"I'm meeting someone."

"Who are you meeting? Maybe I know him."

"I don't think you do."

"Why not?"

"You just don't."

"I've been coming here for years. You never know."

Maybe he did know him. If he was coming for years he might, but even if he wanted to tell him, he didn't have a name so Michael changed the subject: "Why have you been coming for years?"

"Why not? I live around the corner."

"Church Street is close."

"So what?"

"There's lots of places around the corner."

"Why? You don't like this place?"

"It's my second time here."

The big boy got quiet. His face turned red this time. "People can think what they want," he finally said.

"About what?"

"About this place. I met some of the best people I know here."

"Okay."

"Okay, okay," he mocked. "Fuck you." He laughed but it wasn't real. He knew it because he didn't cough after.

"You think you're a wise guy because you go to university. I went to university: U of T. Better than shithole Waterloo."

Michael could've said he was making conversation. That was it. The big boy got him a beer so he was making conversation. It'd probably make things better if he said it, but he didn't want to keep talking anyway. He wasn't here for this so he said nothing.

The guy stopped talking, so Michael pulled his phone out and checked his emails to give him something to do while he waited.

He scrolled through his phone but kept an eye on the guy. The big boy was quiet now but was still a few inches away. Michael thought about going somewhere else to sit but figured it'd make things worse. The guy would probably say something about him moving, so Michael kept going through his phone.

Before he finished his beer the big boy got through his. He got up and told Michael good night. He was acting like a gentleman now. Michael didn't think he'd be nice like that. He was so nice he thought he was going to shake his hand but he left.

Michael sat up to get a good look around. He wanted to make sure the guy didn't just go sit somewhere else—that he actually left. He noticed that the place was getting busier. They were still going with the classic rock, but they played some dance songs too. Michael knew some from when he was a kid. He didn't know the names, but he knew them from hearing them on the radio.

He pretended he was into the music if a song came on that he knew. It gave him something to do. He started moving in his seat as a dance if it was a song he'd heard before. It's not that he liked it but he knew it and it made him more relaxed, being there by himself so that he wasn't just sitting there doing nothing, looking weird.

Someone sat in the seat behind him where the big boy had been, but Michael's back was turned to him so he couldn't see who it was. The guy was sitting close, only a couple of inches. He could feel him staring even though he couldn't see him. Then he said, "I need to catch up." Michael wasn't sure if he was talking to him so he turned a bit to see. All he could make out was the sleeve of a suit. He'd have to turn all the way around to see his face.

"You feel like a shot of tequila?" the guy said.

Michael turned some more. The guy was smiling back at him.

"Me?" Michael said.

The guy pointed right at him. "You."

Michael looked him in the eye. Right in the eye. He tried to remember the eyes. It was him—the guy from last week—it had to be him. It felt like it was. He was older and stockier but handsome.

"I think I've only ever had tequila once," Michael said.

"How about a double tequila? Probably never."

"No, I don't think I've done a double before."

"I need to catch up. Have one with me. I'm buying."

That got Michael smiling.

It felt like it was the guy from last week. If it wasn't him, he liked him anyway, but he was sure it was him.

"Why not?" Michael said. "I'll have one."

"That's the spirit."

The guy introduced himself as "Eddy from Oakville." He said he was downtown most Fridays for the next few months for a work course. He stayed at a hotel across the street. Michael thought of asking if they'd talked last week. He was about to ask, but if they didn't, he didn't want to ruin things. He decided it was better to stay quiet about it and see if Eddy mentioned it first.

After the shot, Eddy bought him a beer. Michael wasn't going to let him because he already got him a drink but Eddy insisted.

They cheersed and Eddy asked, "What things get you going?"

Michael had to think about it.

"Take your time," Eddy said.

"I like to read. I'm studying literature at university."

Eddy thought that was funny. "I wasn't expecting that."

"I read a lot."

"Is that right? You read?"

"I love reading."

"What's your favourite book?"

"*The Call of the Wild*. Jack London." He said it was because of its naturalist themes. Eddy confused "naturalist" with "naturist" and joked that Michael was a nudist. Michael tried to correct him, but Eddy wouldn't let him. He started speaking over him, saying that he was joking; that he was being funny.

"I understand, I understand," Eddy said.

Michael didn't mind being teased. It made it feel like they were close.

He huddled into Eddy so that Eddy would put his hand on his thigh. He knew he'd do that. Then Eddy got his lips near Michael's ear. Michael could smell cologne. It wasn't strong. It was like he'd put it on in the morning. It wore off during the day, but he could still smell it a bit.

"Do you want to get out of here?" Eddy said. He blew in his ear a bit when he said it.

"Sure."

Michael pulled his head back. They were face-to-face. They both smiled; their noses almost touched. They could've kissed if they wanted to. It was better to wait for later, but they could've.

Eddy looked down at his lips. "Can I tell you something?"

"Sure."

"You're the most handsome guy here. Serious. I'm a lucky guy."

"Thank you."

"You're welcome. So, tell me, have you eaten yet?"

Michael had to think. "I was going to get another slice."

"Another slice?"

"Yes."

"Of pizza?"

"Yeah."

"What kind of pizza?" He kept staring at Michael's lips. It looked like he was learning something from them.

"A cheese pizza."

"Cheese pizza?" He said it like he didn't believe it. "Well, we can do better than that. And I'm buying."

"You don't have to."

"I'm buying." His eyes got wide. He said he wouldn't have it any other way.

"Okay," Michael said. "Thanks."

"You can thank my work."

"Thanks, work."

"You're welcome," he said, making his voice sound like a baby's.

He smacked Michael's thigh. "Finish your drink and let's get out of this dump."

Michael drank the rest of his beer.

"Do you like sushi?"

"I'll try it."

"You've never tried it? We're having sushi. I'm going to pop your sushi cherry."

They went to a place that Eddy said had the best sushi in town. It was a two-minute walk down the street from Denim.

When they sat down, Eddy got Michael to tell him more about school. While he was talking, Eddy unwrapped his chopsticks and started pinching Michael's arm with them. He was acting like he was putting pieces of him in his mouth. He never pinched too hard except one time. It made Michael jump, but Eddy winked at him like he meant to do it.

When nobody was looking, Eddy would reach across the table, grab his hand and squeeze. He'd do it for a second, then let go. He'd rub Michael's leg with his foot at the same time. He only did it when no one was looking.

He was twice Michael's age, but in the restaurant, he turned into a little boy. He got this goofy look he didn't get at Denim. Eddy was having fun with him, but Michael didn't mind. He was having fun too. It was the first time he felt good since leaving his parents' place.

The only thing Michael knew on the menu was the photo of the California rolls. He'd seen it before; he didn't know where. He said that that's what he wanted, but Eddy wouldn't let him. It was too boring. That's what Eddy said. He needed something more interesting. He took the menu from him and said he was going to order him salmon maki because it was "real sushi." When the waiter came by, he asked for a squid appetizer too. He told the waiter they'd share it. He also asked for something called *aged tofu*.

When the waiter left, Eddy squeezed Michael's hand, but he didn't let go even if someone passed by, it didn't matter. He held his hand and his face got goofier.

"How many men have you been with?" he asked.

"Not a lot," Michael said.

"You're so beautiful though. How old are you?"

"Nineteen."

"That's why."

"Why?"

"Because you're nineteen."

"How many men have you been with?"

"I'm new to this," Eddy said. "Not many." Silence. "Do you believe me?"

"Yeah."

Eddy let go of his hand and leaned across the table. "I like you a lot," he whispered. It made Michael laugh. "Stop laughing at me," Eddy said. "I mean it."

"I know."

"Do you?"

"I like you a lot too."

"You're just saying it because I said it." He grabbed Michael's hand again but pushed it away, pretending to be mad. He was just acting goofy.

"I do," Michael said.

"You better."

Whether it was the guy from last week, it didn't matter. This was what Michael wanted.

When the squid came, Michael didn't know what to do with it. Most of the pieces had tentacles on them. He didn't think it'd look like what it was.

Eddy started picking at it with his chopsticks before taking a piece.

"They got the best sushi in the city," he said, letting Michael know that he should try it.

Michael picked up a piece with his fingers and threw it into his mouth. Juice gushed out when he bit into it and then it got chewy. It was hard to hide how he felt. Eddy told him to close his eyes and focus on the taste instead of the texture.

Michael tried another. He closed his eyes and pretended that what Eddy said helped. He didn't want him to think he didn't like it.

"Where are you staying tonight?" Eddy asked.

"I don't know."

"You have a home, don't you?"

Michael laughed. "I do. A basement apartment in Kitchener. I might have to take the bus back tonight."

"You can stay at my hotel if you want. It's closer than Kitchener."

"Where's the hotel?"

"A few minutes from here." Silence. "It's an option."

Michael blushed. "I'm up for that."

"Of course you are," Eddy said. He reached across the table and rubbed Michael's hand. Then he grabbed it and shook it in the air like they were champions. It made Michael feel like a champ; he felt he could do anything he wanted. He told himself all week that he was going to find Eddy. There, he found him. Or if it wasn't him, it was someone better.

°

Eddy was staying at the Holiday Inn on Carlton Street. It wasn't far. It was another two-minute walk.

Michael didn't notice the floor he was on. In the elevator they started kissing. He'd thought about kissing him all night and it felt good. They were both a bit drunk. They'd had the drinks at Denim and beers at the sushi place. Eddy also got a bottle of sake. Michael had never tried it, but he liked how it was warm.

When they got to his room, Eddy said he needed to shower. He had to get clean. He hadn't showered since morning. He locked the door in the bathroom behind him.

Michael sat at the edge of the bed and bounced a bit. It was better than the one in Pence's basement. He knew it would be, but he wanted to see how much better it was. He fell back onto the mattress and sunk into it. It was so soft he felt it could eat him. He didn't want to move because of the feeling and fell asleep like that for a couple of minutes, waiting for Eddy to finish showering. It was a light sleep. He didn't even know he was sleeping.

"Enjoying yourself?" Eddy said. He was wrapped in a towel. His chest was tanned and there was no hair anywhere on his body.

Michael opened his eyes and sat up. He smiled. "Yes."

"Maybe a little too much?"

"I'm having an awesome time."

"Awesome. Did I tell you how beautiful you look? I mean it. Don't laugh. You smell nice too. Most guys there don't smell too great. I went there once before. I didn't meet anyone. It's not a nice place, is it?"

"I've only been twice."

Eddy sat next to him and rubbed his thigh. His eyes were on his hands, which moved from his leg to his chest and around his back. Then he started to squeeze his shoulders from the front before kissing him. He did it slow and shut his eyes. Michael kissed him just as slow but his eyes were wide open. He wanted to see Eddy when he did it.

Eddy undressed him as slowly as he kissed him. When he got him naked, he stood back to get a good look.

"Beautiful," he said. He looked him in the eye. "You want to be mine don't you?"

"Anything you want."

"But that's what you want, isn't it?"

"Yeah."

Eddy was careful with his body like it could break. Even when he fucked him, he was careful. He didn't put it in too quick. He went slow and if Michael jumped, he'd pull out and try again even slower.

He kept saying that Michael was his sexy boy.

81

o

Michael woke up the next morning feeling so cozy he couldn't move. He wanted to reach for Eddy, but he closed his eyes again, going in and out of sleep. The feeling of the mattress and duvet stuffed between his limbs did him in.

Michael opened his eyes again a few hours later. It was morning. The sun was coming in between the curtains. The room was quiet; he felt he could go back to sleep. He was about to but lifted his head. "Are you up?" he said.

He moved his leg and tried to find Eddy with his foot. It was just him in bed.

Eddy's suitcase that was sitting open on the loveseat was gone.

Michael threw the sheets off him. He got up and checked the bathroom. The countertop was cleared of toiletries.

He went back to the bed, threw all the sheets on the floor and sorted through them as if Eddy could be wrapped up in them even though it was impossible. He couldn't believe that he would've left like that, but he did. There wasn't a note with a phone number either. Michael checked around the side tables in case it fell.

He checked the bathroom again. He turned the light on to get a good look. The shower was dry. The counter around the sink was covered in water. Eddy must've just washed his face and left. It didn't make sense to Michael that he'd leave like that. It was a good night. It went better than he thought it would. Why leave like that?

Michael didn't know what to do, so he started pulling his clothes out from the sheets on the floor. He made a pile for his clothes, but he couldn't find a sock. He got on his hands and knees and looked under the bed. He was hoping to find a note from Eddy but only found the other sock.

When he started putting his clothes on, he could smell Eddy's aftershave. He pressed his nose against his shirt sleeve—Eddy's smell was stuck in it.

Back on the street, it hit him that he should've tried figuring out Eddy's last name or phone number from the hotel. He wasn't sure if they'd say, but he could've asked. The worst they'd say was no. He was going toward the Greyhound station but turned around. He started walking back to the hotel, but he realized that he didn't pay attention to the room number when he came out or the floor they were on. Even if he went back, what was he going to say? He turned around again and started replaying the whole night in his head. He was trying to make sense of it. There was nothing he could point to and say that that's what went wrong. It made him feel stupid because he felt there was something he wasn't seeing.

When he got to the Greyhound station, he decided he wasn't going home. He wasn't going to let the weekend end like that. Pence would want to do dinner again if he went back. He didn't want to eat with him, and it wasn't just eating. He'd probably want sex too, and Michael didn't want to do that. He'd rather stick around the city another night. Even if he had nowhere to sleep, he could go to the sauna. He could get a room there. He didn't like the place but at least there was a bed. He could go to Church Street, have a good night. If he needed to go the sauna after, that's where he'd go. The only thing he wished was that he'd showered before he left the hotel. He wanted to get out of there. He wasn't thinking, but he needed to wash up.

He had his membership for the YMCA. He'd never gone to a Toronto one, but had a membership and figured he could use the one near the village to wash up.

He asked the kid at the counter if he could get two towels when he was buzzing him in. He didn't pay for towel service but told him he'd give him a dollar a towel. He didn't know if they did that but that's what he offered. The kid gave him two towels for free. He didn't care but said that next time the person at the desk might not give him one. It depended on who was behind the counter.

There was a place he knew that did a good breakfast. Their egg sandwiches were filling and didn't cost too much. Their coffee was always fresh too, so he went there after cleaning up at the YMCA. While he was waiting for his food to come, he got a call from Nathan. He let it ring twice before picking up.

"Hello?" Michael said. He acted like he didn't know who it was.

"Hi. It's Nathan."

"Hey. How are you?"

"Can you talk?"

"Sure."

Nathan got quiet. Michael didn't know if the line cut.

"Can you hear me?" Michael said.

"I can hear you."

"Thanks for calling."

"You're happy to hear from me?"

"Of course."

"Is what you wrote yesterday true?"

"Yeah."

"Why didn't you tell me?"

"We just met."

"So what?"

"I've been trying not to think about it."

"I'm a good listener," Nathan said. "You should've told me."

"Probably."

"So, they just kicked you out?"

"Last week."

"Are you okay?"

"I'm fine."

"It doesn't seem like you're fine."

"I am."

"It's a lot. What about that guy you're living with?"

"What about him?"

"You're not with him."

"No, I told you."

"There's something wrong with that guy. I think he thinks he's with you."

"He's not. But you can't just come by like that. He doesn't like people at his place."

"You gotta get out of there," he said.

"I will in the summer. I need to finish this semester. I can't screw up school."

"Yeah, it's a lot."

Michael was trying to think of what to say next. He hesitated. "I like you. I'm not saying I won't eventually want to date, but my head is—"

"I get it."

"Okay."

"Friends for now?"

"Friends for now."

Michael started crying. He didn't know why. He thought it was stupid. He wiped the tears from his face but didn't make any noise so Nathan wouldn't know.

"Where are you?" Nathan said. "Are you still in Toronto?"

Michael had to clear his throat. "I stayed over at a friend's last night."

"Did you go to Church Street?"

"No. We just went for dinner."

"What did you eat?"

"Sushi."

"I love sushi."

"I thought I'd maybe spend the day in the city and take the bus back later."

"I'm coming up in a couple of hours if you feel like meeting."

"That'd be fun."

"I was invited to a house party in Cabbagetown if you want to come too. As friends. Not my date." He laughed. "Think about it. I should be there by about three. And if you need a place to crash, my folks bought a condo there when I was doing my co-op. It's close to Yonge and Bloor. It's not far from the party."

o

Nathan picked a coffee shop near his condo to meet at. It was a spot he knew, behind the Manulife Centre. Coffees there cost more than other places Michael went to. Nothing was cheaper than five dollars and the workers were dressed in second-hand clothes, stuff from the '90s that looked cooler than anything that Michael had ever owned. They didn't serve drip coffee either. The girl behind the counter said an Americano was the closest thing if he wanted a drip coffee. He'd never heard of it but said he'd try one. They only had one size, too. She showed him—it was more like a medium, so he said it was fine.

He found a seat at the back of the shop. He only had to wait five minutes before Nathan got there. He came right to the back but didn't look at Michael until he was at the table. His face was red; he was blushing about something. It made Michael's face turn red too and his body started heating up. He could feel his neck and back get hot.

"How are you?" Nathan said.

"Good."

"Good."

Michael looked down at his coffee and squeezed the cardboard cup. "I'm sorry again."

"You don't have to say that."

"I just wanted to."

"We're good."

"I am though."

"It's fine."

Michael was starting to sweat—he could feel it on his forehead, and knew he had to say something else to stop it: "I'll explain things better next time."

"I'm a good listener."

"I know," he said, even though he didn't know it.

"Do you need a coffee?"

Michael lifted his cup. "No, I'm good."

Nathan ordered an espresso and walked back with it slowly so it wouldn't spill. It looked funny to see him balance it because the mug was so small, and it made his body look big. When he sat back down, Michael said he was sorry again. He needed to say it one last time, but Nathan ignored it. He asked about his family; he wanted to hear everything about him getting kicked out. Nathan didn't care about the sorry. He said to tell him everything from beginning to end. It's not what Michael wanted to talk about, but he told him everything, starting from when he was kicked out. He felt he owed it to Nathan, but he didn't like thinking about it. It wasn't this beautiful thing. It was ugly. It's why he didn't like talking about it. It was too ugly to talk about, but he owed it to Nathan.

"Coming out isn't the same for people like me," Michael said.

"Like who?"

"Muslims."

"You're Muslim?" Nathan seemed surprised but said, "I thought you might be. How did your mom know to ask?"

"I don't know."

"You don't act gay."

"Yeah, but I am."

"You know what I mean," he said. "And she said you had to get out?"

Michael was only telling him all this because he thought it'd make things better, but he didn't want to keep talking about it. He was tired of it, but he told him. He owed it to him, and Michael wasn't wrong: Nathan changed, hearing him talk. He looked sad and was leaning forward. Michael thought he was going to touch his hand, that's how sad he looked. He didn't want him to touch his hand; not because of that.

"Why did you call that teacher?" Nathan asked.

"I had no one else to call."

"You could've called me."

"I didn't know you then."

"If you knew me, I mean. I don't like that guy."

"It's somewhere to stay."

"You know that he's in love with you, right?"

Michael didn't feel like talking about Pence either, so he didn't say anything.

"If you ever need to get out of there, you can always stay with me," Nathan said.

"What about you?"

"What do you mean?"

"Do your parents know about you?"

"It was fine for me. My mom doesn't care. My dad was funny about it at first but now he's cool. I guess it's different when you're Muslim. I always hear about Muslim kids. It's not right."

Michael wanted to say something about that; he felt he needed to defend himself. He didn't know why. He didn't feel Muslim any-more so he had nothing to defend. He used to be, but it's not who he was now. What Nathan said still got him going, hearing him talk about Islam like that. He didn't like it and it was starting to get him worked up. He wanted to say that it wasn't just Muslims. There were other religions that weren't okay with being gay. Maybe that's what bugged him. It wasn't just Muslims. That's what he wanted to say, but it'd just get him worked up more and he wanted to talk about something else, so he mentioned the party. That calmed him down. He told Nathan he'd go but he wanted to know more about it.

Nathan knew the guy hosting it from a co-op he did two years ago in Toronto. His friend was a lawyer; most people there would be. "A lot of them work on Bay Street," he said. "That's where I did my co-op."

When they finished their coffees, Nathan said they should go get dinner before the party. There was a place he wanted to take him to. He hadn't been there in a while, but he said the food was good, and that he was paying. He said that they needed to celebrate Michael's coming out.

"You don't have to," Michael said. "It's fine."

"It's on me." Nathan laughed when Michael didn't say anything. "It's not a date, so calm down."

That made Michael laugh too because it wasn't what he was thinking.

"Oh, get over yourself," Nathan said, pretending he was whacking Michael across the head.

Michael laughed even harder.

"We need to celebrate. That's it. Are you okay with it?"

"I am. I'm not laughing at you. I'm having fun."

°

They went to Nathan's condo first because he wanted to clean up before dinner. He asked if Michael needed to clean up too, but he said he was fine—he'd already showered and he didn't need another.

The lobby of Nathan's building was all white with pearl-coloured chandeliers hanging high over their heads and white marble floors. The front desk, the other furniture—everything was white. It was like something from a magazine.

Nathan's condo was up on the twenty-sixth floor. It had a view of all the buildings downtown with the CN Tower sticking out behind them. Michael had never seen the city like that, not from that high up, and he kept telling Nathan how nice the view was.

His condo didn't have much in it. Michael didn't say anything about it, but the living room was empty except for a sofa and a

TV on the floor with speakers next to it. The kitchen didn't have a microwave. There was a kettle and a coffee maker, that was it. Nathan noticed Michael noticing and said he was going to move in properly once he finished school. He had a job lined up but said it wasn't the place he did his co-op at. It was a different firm that paid a lot of money, and he could do the condo up nice once he started working. He'd get proper furniture and everything. "It will look cool," Nathan said. He went to the window and looked at the city. "Anyway, it'll take me two seconds to shower. Grab a beer from the fridge if you want."

Michael went to the fridge. There wasn't any food in there, just four different types of beer. He hadn't heard of any of them, so he just picked one and drank it while he watched music videos on his phone.

Nathan came out a few minutes later in a towel. His hair was wet and he didn't have a shirt on. He said he wanted a beer too. Michael watched him go to the fridge. He'd never seen him without a shirt on. He was fit; there was no fat on him, and he had no body hair. There was nothing wrong with the way he looked; it was how people tried to look. It was different from Michael, who had had hair in places he didn't want hair: on his lower back and a bit around his shoulders. He thought he was too thin too. Nathan worked out. His arms were big, he had round pecs, and his waist was small.

"I'll just be five minutes," Nathan said, taking his beer to the bedroom.

House music started coming from the speakers next to the TV. It made Michael jump. It was a slow beat but loud. Nathan must've put it on from his room.

He came back out in jeans and a pressed blue shirt that matched his eyes. Michael figured he'd picked it on purpose because of that. It was tucked in and there were a few buttons at the top that weren't done up so it showed a part of his chest. Seeing how Nathan was dressed made Michael feel that he wasn't

dressed nice enough. He had on the black shirt from yesterday.
There was nothing special about it. Nathan looked like he was
going somewhere special, but Michael felt ordinary in his clothes
and wished that he had something different to wear to the party.

Nathan took him to an Italian place to eat. It wasn't far from
the condo in a part of town Michael hadn't been to. The streets
were small and tidy and everyone was dressed fancy. Nathan said
it was where all the expensive restaurants were and that he wanted
to go somewhere nice because they were celebrating.

Everything on the menu was three times the price of anything
at any restaurant Michael had been to. It was written in Italian too.
They'd explain what things were in English underneath, but even
some of those words Michael didn't know.

Nathan asked if he wanted a cocktail or if they should get
wine. He passed the drink menu to Michael to see, so he went
through it but just looked at the prices. None of the wines were
cheaper than a hundred bucks, and the cocktails were twenty-five
each. For one drink: twenty-five dollars.

"Do you like old fashioneds?" Nathan said.

"What's that?"

"You've never had it?"

"I'll try it."

"Let's get old fashioneds. Wine will put me to sleep. I don't
want to go to sleep."

When the waiter came and asked Michael what he wanted, he
told Nathan to go because he still hadn't picked. Nathan read something Italian off the menu. He didn't try to say it with an accent. It
sounded the way he'd say things in English but it was Italian.

The waiter looked at Michael again so he said, "I'll get the
same."

"It has pork in it," Nathan said.

Michael laughed. "It's okay."

"I thought you're not supposed to eat pork."

"There's a lot I'm not supposed to do."

"Good point."

"Anything else, sir?" the waiter said.

Nathan asked for two old fashioneds too and the waiter went away.

"If there's a hell, I'm going whether I eat pork or not," Michael joked.

"You're not going to hell."

"I guess we'll see."

"You don't think that do you?"

"I don't think so," Michael said. "Why, do you believe in religion?"

"I go to church sometimes. You can be gay at my church. I'm United."

Michael didn't know what that meant but he didn't ask.

"You're not religious then?" Nathan said.

Michael shook his head. "No, but sometimes I have dreams that it's the end of the world and I get scared about going to hell. Because when the world is ending, it's too late to become religious."

"This is a dream you had?"

"It's one I had a few times. The world is going to blow up or something and there's no time to do anything. I get really scared about it because I'm afraid of going to hell but when I wake up I'm not scared anymore."

Nathan started laughing. He wouldn't stop. "That's weird." He had to grab the table tight to get him to stop laughing.

"Sorry," Michael said.

"Don't say sorry. I have weird dreams too. Everyone does."

"I've had that dream a few times."

"If you're going to hell, I'm going to hell."

"I don't think I'm going to hell. I just have dreams about it."

"We'll be friends in hell."

Michael laughed.

"Now I'm being weird," Nathan said.

"It's not that weird."

The waiter brought out the drinks, and Nathan lifted his glass. "To friends in hell."

Michael felt like he could cry; it hit him out of nowhere. He was laughing, and then he felt tears in his eyes. He wasn't sad. He was feeling good. He had to stop himself from crying—even if it was a happy cry, it'd be stupid if he cried.

Nathan looked like he was feeling good too. It wasn't like when they were at school in the cafeteria. He wasn't trying to be anything. He wasn't worried about what he was saying.

Michael stopped himself from crying. "I'm having fun," he said. "I've never been somewhere like this."

"Do you like it?"

Michael nodded.

"I only come here if there's a reason to. The drinks are good."

"They're easy to drink."

"That's the problem. They hit you hard."

The waiter brought the pasta out and put the plate in front of Michael, who started moving his fork through it. It was tube pasta with tomato sauce, mushrooms, and sausage chunks. He licked his fork; he thought the sauce would taste like the ones he got from the store but it was smoky tasting and kind of sweet.

It didn't seem like a lot of food, not for what it cost. Michael thought there'd be more, but Nathan said something about it before he started eating—that it never looked like a lot, but it was more filling than it looked.

The waiter also gave them warm bread that Nathan used to push the pasta onto his fork. He'd eat the pasta, then throw the bread in his mouth. Michael started doing it too. He thought that's how it was to be done.

"Do you want brandy?" Nathan said when they finished eating.

"I'll try it."

A different waiter cleared the table and got them some brandy. It tasted strong but it smelled like plums. Michael drank it slowly like Nathan said—they were only supposed to sip it.

The party had just started so there was no rush—they didn't want to be the first ones there—so they could enjoy the drinks and take their time.

○

They stopped at a corner store before the party. Nathan wanted a Red Bull, so he got one of the big cans and when they were walking, he'd take a sip then pass it to Michael, who'd have some and pass it back. They did it the whole way to the party, passing it back and forth.

Nathan started telling him about the job he was going to start when he was done school. It was at a law firm, but he was working on the business side. He was talking fast, getting excited talking about it. He was shivering too. It was cold and the drink was cold. His teeth were chattering and he kept talking faster.

Nathan said he knew lots of people in Waterloo, but he didn't have gay friends there. Michael was the only one. People like them needed to be in a big city. Michael had to come to Toronto when he finished school—he couldn't come before that. School was important; he was gay; he couldn't drop out. Nathan got serious when he said it. He told Michael he couldn't let what happened with his family stop him from finishing. He made Michael promise he wouldn't drop out. He couldn't show people that gays were nothing.

○

Everybody at the party was dressed like Nathan, in button-down shirts. They were in different colours but they looked the same. The only people not dressed like that were Michael and the bartenders. They had two bars set up in the kitchen and dining room, and the guys behind them weren't wearing any shirts, showing off their bodies.

Nathan got them drinks and they went to the living room, where the DJ was. A few people were dancing but mostly people were standing around and talking. Nathan wasn't saying anything to Michael. He was moving his leg with the music and looking around at everyone. It was mostly guys there; all handsome and clean-cut. There were women but not many. Michael saw two or three.

"I'm going to the kitchen," Nathan said, after not saying anything for a few minutes. "Do you want to come?"

"Yeah, sure."

Michael thought Nathan would know more people there, but it was like he knew nobody and nobody knew him.

He was saying sorry, trying to push through the crowd of people to get to the kitchen. It was hard to get anywhere without pushing, but he found them a spot to stand between the fridge and the bartender.

Nathan was still looking around like he was trying to find someone. Then he said, "How much do you think this house cost?"

Michael didn't know the cost of things like that. It was a nice place, an old Victorian house with high ceilings and a long staircase, but they'd fixed it up to look brand new.

"It's over two million," Nathan said. "I'm not joking. All the homes around here cost that much."

"I didn't know that."

"A lot of them have cottages in Muskoka too. There's a lot of money here." Nathan was about to say something else, but he stopped because this guy was coming over to them. He grabbed Nathan's hand and gave it a good shake. "There you are," he said. "The man of the hour."

"The man of the hour?" Nathan said. "Hardly."

"I was hoping you'd come." He turned to Michael. "Who is this?"

"This is Mike, my best friend from Waterloo."

"You never mentioned him. He's adorable. I'm Rodney," he said, letting go of Nathan's hand and reaching for Michael. He squeezed his hand and shook it hard, like he was trying to ring something out of him, making Michael's body shake.

"It's a great party," Michael said. He didn't know what else to say but it seemed to be the right thing.

Rodney didn't let go of his hand. He was holding it and had his other hand on Michael's back while he talked to Nathan about work stuff. When he let go of Michael, he turned to him and said, "I'm just going to steal Nate for one sec." He smiled. "We'll be back." He pulled Nathan away into the crowd.

Michael didn't like being left alone. He lifted his drink and his lips tried to find the straw. He sucked it down in less than thirty seconds. He turned and asked the bartender behind him for another. He said he wanted a double this time and took it to the living room where the DJ was still playing.

It was getting fuller; more people were dancing.

Michael went to the food table in the back. He wasn't hungry but stood there because it was the only spot where no one else was. He figured he'd wait there for Nathan to come back. It'd be a safe spot.

Someone came out from the crowd and introduced himself. He asked who Michael was, so he mentioned Nathan, that they were friends, thinking he might know him. He didn't, but told him that he was beautiful, admitting that that's why he wanted to talk to him.

The guy started telling him about his cottage and how big it was. He brought it up out of nowhere. It had lots of rooms, he said. It was like a house but made of wood, on a lake in Muskoka. The guy said Michael could come up anytime if he wanted to come. He could bring Nathan too; he asked if they were a thing, but Michael said they weren't, they were friends. The guy said he could bring him anyway. He told him it was nice up north, even in the winter. They could walk on the lake; it'd all be frozen soon. The guy was talking so fast it was like he was talking to himself. Michael hardly said anything. He was going on about the cottage, telling him more stuff about it, and then he mentioned his husband—he said he was about Michael's age, maybe older. He was Latino, and he asked Michael if he was Latino too. He told him no, he was Lebanese. He said he was born here but his parents came from Lebanon. The guy said Michael was beautiful no matter what he was. He rubbed Michael's back when he said it, then whispered in his ear that he needed to find his husband and he was gone.

Someone else came up and started talking to him. He asked some of the same questions about who he was and said he had a cottage too. He didn't invite Michael but told him about it, how it was a log cottage on a lake in Muskoka. They talked for five minutes, but when they had nothing else to talk about, the guy asked if Michael wanted some coke. He pulled out a small baggie from his pocket to show him. Michael thanked him but said he was okay right now—he'd never done anything like that but didn't want to start. The guy rubbed Michael's back and said if he changed his mind to find him.

More people came. They all wanted to know who he was, and some tried to push more coke onto him. He said thank you but no and he had to keep saying it because more people asked if he wanted some.

He watched for Nathan the whole time. He didn't want to keep doing this all night—he was getting tired talking to all these people and having the same conversation over again. He wanted to get out of there. Maybe they could go to Church Street after, to some bar there. It'd be more fun. He'd been to a couple of bars there, but there were some places he hadn't been. It'd be better to go somewhere new than stay. People were nice but he was getting tired of this.

Michael went to the kitchen for another drink. He thought Nathan might be there, but it was hard to tell people apart—the lights were down lower than before, and it was filled with guys. It was hard to move too, and the music was louder. There was a disco ball hanging from the ceiling that he didn't notice before and the lights from it made the room look like it was spinning.

There was a line to get a drink now, so Michael joined it and checked his phone. Nathan hadn't called, so he tried calling him but there was no answer. He texted instead of leaving a message, asking where he was.

The guy behind him was saying something. Michael sent the message and turned around.

"Sorry, were you talking to me?" Michael said.

"You look like you're having as much fun as I am," the guy said. He had an accent. It sounded American: somewhere in the south, but he didn't know where from.

Michael smiled. "It's my first time."

"Run!" The guy chuckled. It was a loud chuckle; it didn't sound real. "Don't come back."

He was dressed like everyone else, but his face was rough; he looked like he could cut a rock with his face. The guy tilted his head to the bartender. "There's a lineup for the bathroom and now to get a drink. Where the hell are we?"

Michael laughed. It was true; he didn't get it either. "Why are there lines everywhere?"

"Goddammit."

The line moved a bit.

"God damn line," the guy said. "I should stop coming to these things. They keep inviting me and I keep coming."

"Why?"

"The short story is I just moved to the neighbourhood. They keep inviting me so I come."

"Do you have nothing else to do?"

"I guess not," he laughed. "There's a lot of change in my life right now."

Michael's phone started ringing. "Just a second," he said. "My phone." He pulled it from his pocket. It was Nathan. "I should get this."

"I'll be waiting here," the guy joked.

"Where are you?" Michael said.

People were laughing on the other end of the phone. All he could hear was laughing.

"Are you there?" Michael said. "Where are you?"

There was more laughing. Then Nathan said, "I'm upstairs." He was laughing now too. "Where are you?"

"I'm getting a drink," he said.

"Where?"

"In the kitchen. There's a lineup."

"Come upstairs," he said.

"I'll get a drink and come up."

"We're in the bedroom."

"Do you want me to get you a drink?"

"A double."

"A double what?"

"Double vodka soda, buddy. Please. And tell the bartender he's hot."

Someone grabbed the phone from Nathan. "He so fuckin' hot," they said.

Michael hung up.

"Is your friend okay?"

"He's upstairs," Michael said.

"Sounds like trouble."

It was his turn for a drink. "I think he'll be okay if I get him one of these."

"I'll be down here if you need me."

He took the drinks upstairs to one of the bedrooms. There were about twenty people sitting around with their shirts off. Someone was playing music from their phone: a tribal remix of a Lady Gaga song.

Michael found Nathan sitting on the side of the bed topless, talking to someone with his shirt off too.

"Mike!" he said. "This is my best friend from Waterloo. He's such a nice guy."

Everyone looked over at Michael, even people who were talking to other people.

"Hi everybody," Michael said. It was all he could think to say. "Here's your drink."

"Aw, take your shirt off, Mike," Nathan said, standing up. He took both drinks from his hands, put them on the nightstand, and tried to take Michael's shirt off.

"No, no, no, please," Michael said. He started laughing but crossed his arms over his chest. "Maybe later."

"Come on, it's the rule," Nathan said. "No shirts past midnight."

"It's not midnight yet."

"No shirts past midnight," he said again.

Nathan was out of it. His eyes weren't right. Michael hadn't seen him like that before, and he thought maybe he'd done coke. He didn't want to ask; it wasn't his business. If he did it, he did it, but he looked out of it.

"Everyone will have their shirt off in an hour," Nathan said.

"It's what we do," someone else said. "I don't know why though. Why do we do it?"

"I don't know."

Nathan wouldn't let up. He kept trying to take his shirt off so Michael let him. He lifted his arms and Nathan pulled it off. Everyone clapped like it was a big deal, and the guy next to him rubbed his chest. "I like your fur," he said. Michael was the hairiest one there. There was only one other guy who had hair on his chest, but it was trimmed. There was too much hair for Michael to trim without it looking off.

"I got nothing," Nathan said. "Feel it. I got nothing." He grabbed Michael's hand and used it to rub his chest. His skin was warm and was covered in sweat. "It's like a baby's ass."

"Like a baby's bottom, you mean," someone said, imitating a British accent.

Nathan laughed, letting go of Michael's hand and pinching the nipples of the guy next to him. "Bastard."

Nathan finished his drink quickly. Even after he was done, he kept sucking at the straw, making noise. Michael wasn't sure if he was doing it to be funny or if he didn't notice it was empty. Then he stopped and said, "I need to go to the bathroom."

"I'll come with you," Michael said.

Nathan laughed. "You want to pee with me, don't ya? Don't ya?"

"Oh, shut up," Michael said. He grabbed Nathan by the arm and pulled him off the bed.

There was a line for the toilet. Nathan tried to go right to the front, but Michael grabbed him. He said they had to wait. "There's a line."

"You're so hairy," Nathan said, looking at his chest.

"I know."

"I have nothing."

"I know."

"Do you like hairy? Are you into bears?"

"I'm good either way."

"Me too," he said.

He started dancing to the music coming from downstairs. "I want to start singing."

"Don't," Michael said. He put his hand over his mouth.

"I'm going to start singing."

"You're crazy."

"Are you having fun?"

"I am."

"It's so much fun."

"I think I'm getting tired, though."

This made Nathan sad. "No, you're not having fun?"

"I am. I didn't sleep well last night."

"You want to go?" He thought Nathan was going to start crying.

"I might. But you stay."

That made him happy again. "Is it okay if I stay?"

"Yeah."

"Are you sure? I don't want to leave you."

"For sure. You stay. I'll be okay."

"You got the key to my place. Go back. Grab a beer if you want. There isn't much food in the fridge if you're hungry. But are you sure?"

"I'm sure. Have fun."

Nathan gave him a kiss. It was on the lips but he didn't use his tongue. He smiled and rubbed Michael's chest. "You're so hairy."

Michael waited until it was his turn for the bathroom and left him there.

o

The streets around the house were quiet. There was a bit of snow falling but not much—he could only see it when it fell under a streetlamp. It was so quiet, it was hard to think there was a party going on in the house where he came from. He couldn't hear anything from the street.

He had to use his phone to figure out where he was. He hadn't been watching when Nathan took him there, but his phone said that Church Street wasn't far—just fifteen minutes away. He'd go to Church for a drink or two but wouldn't stay long—that's what he was saying to himself, to go for a couple of drinks.

He didn't see anyone until he got to Jarvis Street. It got busier there and the snow was coming down even more. The snowflakes were big, but they were falling slowly, like ash.

Michael was the sort of drunk where he didn't know how drunk he was. He knew he wasn't normal, but it wasn't crazy. He went to the bar he ended up in after Denim last week and asked for a vodka shot with his beer because he wanted to be really drunk. He thought it'd pick him up a bit too. He did the shot and found a spot to sit with his beer in the back.

The bar was busy like it was when he was there last. There was a drag show going on that he could see from where he was sitting.

The drag queen was dressed like Whitney Houston and was pretending to sing the song from the *Bodyguard* soundtrack. Halfway through, she pulled a silver compact from her pocket. She opened it when the song picked up and powder—pretend cocaine—went all over her clothes and face. That got the crowd going—they were cheering and started singing with her, word for word.

Michael finished his beer in ten minutes, but he wasn't ready to go. It was like he just got there so he went back to the bar for another drink. While he was waiting for his turn, he thought he saw Eddy on the other side of it. It looked like Eddy; it had to be him. Michael walked around to get a good look—he didn't know what he was going to say if it was him. He was going to say something, but he didn't know what.

When he got around the bar, he saw that it wasn't Eddy. Not the Eddy from yesterday. It was the real Eddy. The one from Denim. The first one from last week. His name probably wasn't Eddy; whatever his name was, it was him.

Michael got a closer look: seeing him again, he remembered. Whoever he was with yesterday at the hotel was someone else—it's not who he'd met at Denim originally. He'd confused the two and slept with the wrong one. The real Eddy was waiting for a drink, so Michael went up and said hello. The guy didn't hear him; he was watching the drag show while he was waiting so Michael said hello again. He turned and smiled the way Michael remembered him smiling. "Hi there."

"How are you?"

"Better now." The guy used his whole face to smile; his face wrinkled up and it made him look older. "I didn't think I was going to see you again."

"Do you remember me?" he said.

"Of course I do. From last week."

"Yeah, from last week."

"I've never seen someone run so quickly. I must've given you a fright."

The bartender pointed at the real Eddy and asked what he wanted.

"I'm going to get my friend here a drink," he said. "What can I get you?"

"Just a beer," Michael said.

"You have to be more specific," the bartender said.

"A Keith's."

"Keith's and two rum and Cokes." He turned to Michael. "What's your name?"

"Mike."

"Hi, Mike. I'm Troy. Will you come and have a drink with me and my friend?"

"Sure."

Michael followed him to the front of the bar. There weren't as many people up there. Everyone was in the back watching the drag show. In the front, there were big round tables made of wood with wooden chairs. They were all taken, but it wasn't busy like in the back.

Troy took him to one of the tables that had this young guy waiting there. He was younger than Michael and thin, like his bones were trying to push out of his skin—he looked sick. He had a Beyoncé belly top on, showing off his rib cage.

"That took forever," the young one said. "I need to go for a smoke." He got up and grabbed his drink from Troy. He sucked on the straw, drinking half of it at once, then gave it back.

"Phil, Mike. Mike, Phil."

"Who?"

"Mike." He pointed at Michael. "He's a friend."

"He's cute," he said. He looked Michael up and down. "I need a smoke. I'll be back."

"Please, sit down," Troy said to Michael.

"Is everything okay?" Michael asked.

"Of course."

"Was he mad?"

"Why would he be?"

"I don't know." Michael took a seat. "Who is he?"

"I've known that one for too long. I can't even remember how long." He lifted his glass. "Cheers."

Michael raised his glass too.

"I met that one when we were living in Brampton. That's how long it's been. I've been downtown now for years. Are you from here?"

"Um, I go to school in Waterloo but live in Kitchener. I'm staying with a friend here tonight. We were at a party before this." He took a sip of beer and looked up at the drag queen. She still had powder all over her but was singing a song that Michael hadn't heard before.

"Are you okay?" Troy said.

"Yeah."

He smiled and rubbed Michael's leg. "Do you go to Denim a lot?"

"I've been twice."

"So I was lucky to meet you there?"

"I guess so."

"That's where I met Phil. He's a good kid even though sometimes he's not." He laughed.

"Are you guys together?"

"No, no. We fuck around sometimes. That's it." Silence. "Is that okay?"

"Yeah."

"What do you think of him?"

"What do you mean?"

"Is he your type or are you only into daddies?"

"I don't know."

"It doesn't bug me, people calling me Daddy. The first time someone said it, it did but not anymore. Young guys like it, I don't know why."

"I don't think I have a type," Michael said.

"Life is too short to have a type."

"I guess."

"Phil's got the fattest cock you've ever seen." Troy laughed. "Seriously. He's so skinny. I tell him that he looks like he's on drugs. He needs to put on a bit of weight, but that cock: I don't know where it came from."

Michael squeezed his beer glass. He was trying not to be bothered but was squeezing it as hard as he could.

"We're going to go back to my place for a drink if you want to come. I'm not far."

Michael looked down at the glass but kept squeezing. "I'm feeling really tired."

"It's Saturday night. You got all week to sleep. Come on, just come for a drink. I think Phil liked you. And he loves having his dick played with."

"He's not my type," Michael said.

"Oh. Well, I'll tell him to go home so it's just you and me. He won't mind. Is that what you want?"

"I don't know."

"I think it is what you want." He came closer to Michael. "Can I ask you a question?"

Michael hesitated. "What?"

"Can I kiss you?" He didn't wait for Michael to answer. He started kissing him. They were so close, it'd be hard to stop him. Michael didn't like the feeling of it right away—there were a lot of feelings, and he didn't like any of them, but Troy kept kissing him and grabbed the side of his body with his hand. He got a good grip and pushed into him more. Michael started kissing him back; it was the only thing he could do, but kissing him like that made Michael forget what Troy was talking about before. His body relaxed with the way Troy was grabbing him. It wasn't right, but he was starting to like it. He thought he was dumb for liking it, but it made him feel good.

Troy squeezed his body harder. The sounds of the drag show disappeared. It was like they were somewhere else. Whatever

Michael was thinking before about Troy was gone. His head got quiet.

Troy grabbed Michael's dick and pulled his head back. "Fuck," he said. "I bet that fat cock is dripping, isn't it?"

Phil was back at the table. He was staring at them. "Is he coming home with us?"

"I hope so," Troy said. He let go of him. "Are you?"

Phil was sipping his drink and watching the drag queen.

"Or do you want him to leave?"

"I don't know."

"Have you ever been watched? Phil is a pervert—he likes to watch."

"No."

"He can watch but if you don't like it, he can go."

"Okay."

"Finish your drink," he said.

Phil started telling Troy about someone he was talking to outside. He said they knew each other, but they couldn't figure out from where. They asked each other a bunch of questions, and it turned out they went to elementary school together. Phil thought it was funny, and Troy started laughing too.

When Michael finished his beer, he said he needed to go to the toilet and that he wouldn't take long. Troy kissed him and made him promise to come back.

Michael went toward the bathroom but kept going to the other side of the main bar. He pushed through the crowd that was now watching a different drag queen who'd gotten up on stage. She was older and was in a yellow sequin gown.

He left the bar through a side exit. He walked quickly so Troy and Phil wouldn't see him and kept going down the street. He started running for two blocks, then looked behind him to make sure nobody was following him and went back to Nathan's place.

o

Michael woke up close to noon. He turned his head and could see the downtown skyline from the sofa where he was sleeping. The clouds were over the buildings, covering the top of the CN Tower. It looked like it was going to rain.

When he sat up, he thought he'd feel worse than he did. He drank a lot but not like Friday. It was almost like he didn't drink because of how fine he felt. Even when he stood up he felt fine.

He went to Nathan's room. The door was open so he came close and slowly peeked in. Nathan was sitting up in bed on his phone but put it down when he noticed Michael. "My head hurts," he said. "I can't see straight. How about you?"

"I feel okay," Michael said.

"Did you have fun?"

Michael went to the bed and lay next to Nathan over the covers.

"It was a good time," he said.

"It was a fun party. They liked you a lot."

"They were really nice."

Michael put his head down on the pillow. The sheets smelled like soap, the one Nathan used. "It's weird. I feel fine. I drank so much."

"I wish I felt fine."

They lay there; they didn't say anything. Michael almost fell asleep again.

"You still alive?" Nathan said.

He couldn't see him because of the covers. "I think so."

"Good."

Michael closed his eyes again. "Can I ask you a question?"

"Sure."

"Are we best friends?" Michael said.

"You're the only one from Waterloo who knows I'm gay."

"Really?"

"I told you that, but I don't care who knows. I just don't advertise it."

"I never had a best friend. I was always by myself. Even when I was a kid, I was alone. You don't think that's weird?"

"Some people are like that."

"Really?"

"You're an introvert. That's okay."

"Okay."

"If you want to be, we can be best friends."

"I do want that."

o

Nathan dropped Michael off in front of Pence's place close to two. He was quiet coming in. He turned the lock slowly and squeezed the handle so it wouldn't make any noise. He took his shoes off, untying the laces first. Instead of walking, he slid his socks across the floor and almost got to the stairs of the basement, but Pence came out of the kitchen.

"Where have you been?" he said.

"Hi. Good morning."

"It's not morning."

"Oh, right. Sorry. I was in Toronto."

"Doing what?"

"I went to a party. With Nathan."

Pence raised his eyebrows. "Things are back on with him?"

"We're just friends."

"You're not a very good liar, are you?"

"We're just friends."

"You didn't see my texts? I was messaging you all weekend."

"I was going to respond."

"I was starting to worry."

"You don't need to worry."

"I do worry."

"You don't need to worry!" Michael shouted, giving Pence a fright. He didn't mean to shout. It just came out, but it was like it made Pence shrink, having never heard Michael yell like that. His eyebrows shrunk and so did his lips. He wouldn't look at Michael and seemed timid like a child.

"I do worry," he said, almost whispering. "I promised to take care of you. Just call next time if you're going to be away all weekend."

"Fine."

"Is that too much to ask?"

"I can do that."

Michael thought he was going to say something else but Pence was done. Michael continued to the stairs and went down. Pence closed the door behind him. He didn't slam it. He just closed it slowly.

Michael didn't know how much sleep he got last night. He figured he'd try to get some more so he turned the light off and put his head on the pillow. He was out in two seconds. When he opened his eyes again it was dark outside the windows, and he couldn't see anything. His stomach was hurting too. The only food he'd had was when Nathan stopped at the Tim Hortons drive-thru on the way back for coffee and breakfast sandwiches.

He got out of bed and went up the stairs. Before opening the door, he sat on the last step. He put his ear near the door and listened but couldn't hear anything so he opened it slowly.

The lights were off in the kitchen, but he could now hear Pence talking in the living room. He wasn't far; he could see the light around the corner, coming from the TV. He thought someone else was there with him, so Michael moved closer to the living room until he was on the other side of the wall. He put his ear close to the door, but it was just Pence's voice so he figured he was on the phone, talking to someone.

He was going to go back to the kitchen and make something to eat but he heard his name.

"No, Michael is still sleeping. You'd think he'd grow out of this . . . Yeah, I'm sure it's been hard for him, but life's hard for us all . . .

That's true. Fine . . . No, of course, it was a good idea . . . That might be true, but I couldn't," he said, lowering his voice, "I couldn't let him stay in the closet. If I didn't do something, he'd think he was straight, and we both know what that's like . . . No, I called from a payphone . . . Yes, there are still payphones . . . His mom wouldn't know who it was . . . No, no, believe me, he'll be okay. Even if he knew that I told her, he'd thank me . . . Look, it's fine."

o

Michael wanted to tell Nathan everything that had happened with Pence: how he said he could stay but then made him do the other stuff. He was about to tell him the morning after the party when they were in bed. It almost came out, but he couldn't say it. He was worried that Nathan wouldn't talk to him again if he knew that part. He didn't want Nathan to see him like that.

Even though he wanted to tell him everything when he saw him the next weekend, he only told him about how Pence called his mom. Nathan got mad. They were having drinks at a bar on Church, a place Michael hadn't been to. When he told him, Nathan said he had to get out of there and could stay on his couch until he figured things out. "If I ever see that fuckface, I'm going to sock him one," Nathan said. "What a piece of shit."

o

If he told Pence he was moving out, he'd make a big deal of it. He'd probably start shouting, so Michael thought it was better to leave in the middle of the night. He only had one suitcase anyway. It was an easy move. Nathan came after midnight and helped him.

He slept on Nathan's couch for the rest of the semester. It was comfy and it was in a den, so it was out of the way. He kind of had his own space, and Nathan didn't mind it. His roommate didn't mind either. He was usually at his girlfriend's place.

Nathan said he'd get him a job in the summer, working at a firm he used to work at in Waterloo. It'd pay more than the grocery store and he was sure they'd hire him. He'd be on the couch until then, but with the job he could get his own place. It'd also let him save so he wouldn't need to work during school. He made Michael promise he was going to finish school.

Michael knew Pence would try to find him. From the minute he left, he knew he wasn't done with him, and it didn't take long. Only three days after he left, Pence showed up at school. Michael was going to class, and Pence was there waiting outside the building where he used to drop Michael off at when they'd first met.

When he saw Michael coming, he didn't wait for him to get there. He met him halfway. His skin was pale, not like it usually was. He looked like a ghoul; he was white but his eyes were smudged red. He tried to say something but stopped. He ran his hand through his hair. "Who do you think you are?" Silence. "I took care of you, and this is how you treat me?"

Michael wanted to punch him in the face. He'd never punched anyone before. He didn't know if he should go for the nose. He thought maybe it would kill him, going for the nose. He didn't want to kill anyone, not even Pence, so he thought the cheek would be better. He knew the temple would probably kill him too. It'd have to be the cheek.

Michael stared at his white face. He looked so stupid, Michael smiled. That made Pence madder.

"Say something," he said. "Wipe that smile off your face. What's wrong with you?"

Michael grabbed him by the arm. He couldn't punch him, but he dug his fingers into his skin. He did it hard enough that he knew he was hurting him. A punch would be too much. He could go to jail with a punch.

"Let go of me. What are you doing?"

"I know what you did," Michael said.

Some students passed. They were staring, but Michael didn't care.

"And what did I do?" Pence shook his arm, but Michael wouldn't let go.

"You know."

Pence was about to say something. His pale face turned red like his eyes. He knew. "You're going to thank me someday."

Michael let go of him. "Don't try to find me."

"Or what?"

"You don't want to know."

"Are you threatening me?"

"I'll kill you. Now fuck off." He spit but missed him. He didn't think he deserved his spit anyway.

4

When Michael finished school, Nathan helped him find work in Toronto. He knew lots of people and got him something at an ad agency on King Street. He wasn't in love with the job, but it paid more than he thought it'd pay. He didn't think he'd make that much so young and be able to rent his own place with no roommates. It was a bachelor so it wasn't big, but it was his own, only five minutes from Nathan's off Church Street.

Everyone at Michael's work was serious about the job. It's not that he wasn't. He worked hard and stayed late if he needed to, but he didn't care the way they did. He found it hard to care about something like advertising. The people there acted like it was art and read ad magazines in their free time. They'd paint the whole city in ads and put them on all the sidewalks and across skyscrapers if they could—they'd say stuff like that.

There was something about advertising that bugged Michael; it was like they were tricking people for a living. He never told anyone that that's how he felt. It paid well, and they threw good parties. They were open bar and they'd rent out a whole pub or nightclub for them.

His boss, Dylan, was gay—that was the other good thing. He was Nathan's friend; it was how Michael got the job. They went for coffee every day. His boss would sometimes talk about work but he'd talk about gay stuff too: people he was dating or circuit parties he wanted to go to. He didn't have a problem talking about drugs or sex, and Michael didn't mind. He liked that he could talk to his boss about this stuff. It made the job more fun. He liked his boss, and his boss defended him. Even if Michael made a mistake, if it was his fault, his boss wouldn't say anything bad about him to other people. When they were by themselves, he'd teach him not to do it again, but in front of people he'd defend him.

Michael didn't love the work, but he was happy. His boss was nice and it paid well so he could do stuff. Not like in school, where he was careful about money. He didn't worry about that. Life could be worse.

Every week, usually on a Thursday, he'd meet Nathan, and they'd go somewhere to eat. Not an expensive place but not cheap and they didn't worry about the cost. They'd have food then go for drinks on Church Street. Then one night during the weekend, they'd go together to a gay club in the village. It'd be a Friday or Saturday, and the other night, Michael would do something on his own. He didn't mind going out without Nathan because when he was alone he'd usually meet some guy. He'd never meet anyone with Nathan, but by himself, he met lots of guys who he'd hook up with. It'd usually be a one-off—he'd never start dating the ones he slept with. It's not that he didn't want to be with someone. He did but he didn't meet anyone he wanted to be with more than a night.

o

Nathan started seeing someone, and Michael knew it was serious because he wanted them to meet. He never wanted Michael to meet anyone he was seeing. They'd only been dating a month, but he said it was different. The guy was young but he was smart and was studying at the University of Toronto on a scholarship. The university paid for everything, even where he was living and his food—Nathan told him this so Michael would know he was different from other guys he saw. Nathan was always smiling and making jokes after he met him. It's not that he didn't smile before, but now it was all the time and Michael figured it was because of the guy.

Nathan had made a reservation at a place on Yonge Street for Thursday night so they could meet. Michael went home first, after work, to wash up. The restaurant wasn't far from home, so he figured he'd shower in case they were going to go out somewhere after.

When he got home, in the lobby of the building, he heard someone say his name. He was going for the elevator. He was in a rush; he didn't want to be late. There were a few people in the lobby. He didn't see who said it, but he knew the voice. He looked around and heard it again: "Michael?"

He stopped and turned. It was his mom. He thought his eyes were playing tricks. It'd been years since he'd seen her. She looked smaller than he remembered. She didn't look any older, just smaller; she'd lost weight. She wore a hijab in a floral print. It made her face look tiny. It was wrapped in a way he'd never seen: it was like she spun it in circles around her head instead of wrapping it evenly on both sides.

She smiled, then she started to cry. He didn't say anything to her.

She came closer and wiped her face. She kept crying, waiting for him to say something.

The elevator opened. Some people were getting off, so he got on and pressed the button to close the door. She didn't try to stop him. She watched the doors close between them.

He didn't think she'd be there. How'd she even know where he lived?

He got off two floors below his in case she was watching to see what floor he was on. He didn't want her to know. He took the stairs up to his place and closed the door behind him. He was feeling sad seeing his mom cry, but mad too, because why was she there, showing up out of nowhere?

Michael went into the kitchen, got a bottle of wine from under the sink, and poured a glass. He drank a bunch at once and poured more.

His phone started ringing. It made him jump; he almost spilled his wine. The call was coming from the intercom downstairs so he ignored it and took the wine to the bathroom.

Before getting into the shower, he started texting Nathan. He was writing out that he was going to be late and just as he sent it, his phone started ringing again. He thought about turning it off. He could've, but he didn't. He wanted her to keep calling. He didn't want to answer but he wanted her to call so he could not answer.

He got in the shower and made it hot. It stung at first but he got used to it.

He washed and listened to her call again and again. She didn't stop calling. He was in the shower for ten minutes and she called four times.

He got out and dried himself. She'd stopped calling; the apartment was quiet. He kept drinking wine while he dressed himself. He put his underwear on, then his shirt and pants. He was pretending the calls didn't happen because they'd stopped, but when he was doing his hair in front of the mirror, he said that if she called again, he'd answer. He made it out like she'd earned it if she called one more time.

He was melting hair paste in his hands, rubbing them together to get it warm when the phone rang again. He couldn't pick it up because of the paste. He said that if it was still ringing by the time he washed the paste off, he'd pick up.

He washed them.

It kept ringing.

He dried them and it was still ringing so he picked up.

"Yeah?" he said. "What do you want?"

It was quiet. "I'm sorry," his mom said. It was echoey from the intercom. She was still crying.

"There are people here, habibi," she said. "Please, let me come up."

He drank some wine but didn't say anything; he was trying to think.

"There are people waiting, habibi," she said.

Silence.

"1206," he said, buzzing her up. "You can only stay for five minutes."

How it happened was hard to remember. She knocked on the door. He waited a couple of seconds before opening, then she was inside on the sofa. It was the sofa Nathan gave him. Nathan got a new one. He said he could have it and didn't ask for any money. He just gave it to him, and she was sitting on it now, crying.

She was saying stuff. He didn't ask questions about what she was saying. She was talking about a therapist. She said it like it was nothing. "My therapist said you didn't choose to be this way. She said you're born this way." She kept crying but he didn't say anything. She wanted to talk so he let her.

She said how he looked like a man now. He didn't ask what she meant. He wasn't asking questions.

Seeing how she was crying got to him. It made him feel like he could cry too.

She said sorry a lot and said she'd made a mistake—she didn't know what she was doing. She was Lebanese. It was new to her. She said she didn't sleep properly anymore: not one full night since he left. He remembered that because that's when he started crying too. He remembered trying to hide it, but it was too much. He couldn't stop.

They were hugging. He didn't know who hugged who. It made him cry more. He said sorry. She was saying it so much, he started saying it.

He gave her his phone number and said he'd go to Kitchener to have dinner at the house. She'd asked him. That's why he said it and he promised her because she didn't believe he would.

She kissed him on the cheek and held his face, wiping the tears from it. She kissed him again, then she was gone.

5

Michael asked Nathan if he should go for dinner at his parents'
place. Nathan said everyone should get a chance to prove themselves, but only one chance. "Go once and see," he said. He offered
to go with him, but Michael didn't need that. He was okay alone,
but he understood what Nathan was saying. He'd go and if he
didn't like it, he wouldn't go again.

Nathan offered to drive him to Kitchener so he took him up on
that part. Nathan wanted to visit friends in Waterloo anyway and
would pick him up when he was done. Michael asked that he drop
him off at the end of the street. He didn't say why, and Nathan
knew not to ask. Michael gave him the address to pick him up
from the house when he was done.

Michael got out of the car and thought how the street was exactly how he remembered it when he was walking away the night he was kicked out. It brought all the feelings back from that day. He didn't need them back; he didn't like the feelings. He'd forgotten about them; they were all out of him and now they were coming back.

He went up to the front door and the only thing different was the doorbell. It was big, black, and had a camera on it. He pressed it and it did nothing for a second, but then it started to play a song that sounded like something from a kid's toy.

His dad opened the door. "Hey man," he said. "Long time no see." His dad hugged him and smelled like he always smelled. He bought his aftershave from the pharmacy. That hadn't changed.

His mom came out from the kitchen. She smiled at the sight of them hugging.

"Where have you been, man?"

"Around."

"Your mom said you're a working man now." He smacked his back.

He didn't remember telling her that; he didn't not say it, but he couldn't remember.

"Yeah, I'm working," he said. "It's been six months."

"Good man."

"I want a hug," his mom said, reaching out for him. "I'm glad you came." She whispered it like it was a secret.

They went into the kitchen, which had been redone. The floors were all wood, the counters were marble, and the kitchen table was new. There were some things that were the same: the stove, fridge, and the curtains. It was like a dream where enough was the same that he knew it was the same place but a lot of it was different.

The food was already out on the table. It was a lot of the stuff he ate when he lived at home: stuffed grape leaves, meat pastries, and lentil soup. They were things he couldn't get in Toronto. The Lebanese food near him was all shawarmas and falafels, and there was hummus and baba ganoush in the grocery stores, but it was impossible to get home cooking like this. It was the only thing making him feel good about being back.

His mom asked him to sit down. He told them they only had two hours, that he couldn't stay long because he had work to do, but he just didn't want to stay long in case he didn't like it.

He took the seat at the end across from his dad, who wanted to know more about work. Michael told him what he did but said it wasn't the best job but it wasn't the worst. The pay was decent. His dad said the pay was the most important part. The economy wasn't good. "If you have a job, hold onto it, man."

Michael didn't agree or disagree. He listened to his dad talk some more about the economy and watched his mom take things off the table and reheat them on the stove.

She had blond highlights in her hair that he was only just noticing. It looked like she'd straightened it too. Whenever she'd lean over the table to pick something up, it'd fall to the side and she'd pull it back behind her ears.

His dad was still talking about work, but his work, and still going on about the bad economy. He could always talk, go forever, and his mom let him. He kept going on even after they started eating. Michael thought they were going to talk about everything that had happened the day he left. It's why he was nervous about coming, but it never came up. After his dad was done, his mom brought up his cousins—she said they all missed him—and she told him what they'd all been up to since they saw him last. They also talked about where Michael was living, and whether he liked being in Toronto. His dad brought up his work and the economy again, but the whole dinner, they never talked about the day he left. Michael didn't know if it was good or bad, but it helped him relax. It seemed easier to do that, because what was the point of talking about it? It happened. It wasn't going to unhappen. They were sorry for it. He could see they were sorry in how much food his mom made, and he didn't want to talk about it either.

Michael wasn't sure if they were going to ask whether he was seeing someone. He figured it'd come up since it'd been about five years, but they didn't ask. He wasn't sure if that was good or bad either. It was easier.

His mom made dessert: mafroukeh with cream. He hadn't had it since before he left. He ate two slices then said that he had to go. Nathan had texted him. He was waiting out front by then. His mom looked out the window and could see Nathan's car, but she didn't ask who it was. She said that she hoped they could do it again.

He started coming every third Sunday and it was always like that first time. There'd be lots of food—his mom would cook all day. His dad would talk about work and the economy, but they wouldn't talk about other things. They'd pretend everything was fine, but he'd never stay the full day. He'd be there long enough to make them happy and feel like he was trying.

○

A couple of months in, his mom asked if he could come in the morning on Sunday instead of the evening for dinner. They'd only been doing dinners, but his parents were going to a wedding in the afternoon so he said he could come earlier to eat. He took the Greyhound up but forgot to bring a book, so he was playing around with his phone instead, checking Facebook and Instagram. He was on the gay apps too. He hardly used them but he was bored and the bus was stopped in traffic.

Halfway to Kitchener, he got a message from this guy who he thought he'd seen before. He couldn't remember from where, but he knew his face. It could've been at a party or bar. He couldn't remember. He could've just seen him on Church Street.

The guy wrote *Hey*, and Michael said *Hey* back and *How are you?*

Good, u?

Michael said he was on his way to his parents' place but was hungover; he went out last night. Seeing his parents was the last thing he wanted to do with how he was feeling.

Nice, the guy said. That was it—maybe Michael was being too honest and it turned him off. Michael had nothing left to say either, so he went back to Instagram, and by the time he got to Kitchener, he'd forgotten that they'd even talked.

Michael's dad was waiting for him at the station dressed in a suit. His truck smelled of aftershave and he had a bit of dried shaving foam on his neck. His dad asked how he was and turned the radio down so he could hear him. He didn't drive away. They were just sitting in the parking lot while Michael told him that everything was fine. He didn't say his head was hurting because he drank too much last night.

His dad stayed there parked.

"Is everything okay?" Michael said.

"What do you say we go to the mosque, man?"

"Why?"

"Just to go, man. Just the boys. No women allowed."

Michael wanted to say no, but before he could, his dad mentioned that it was Father's Day—that's why he wanted to go. "It'd be the best present."

"What, today is?"

"It is, man. What do you say? Just the boys? It'd be the best present."

Michael couldn't say no—not if it was Father's Day—so he said he'd go, but he didn't like it. He hadn't been to the mosque since way before he'd left home. Even before leaving home, he didn't ever go. His dad didn't go either. He couldn't remember him going. If there was a reason to go on a Friday, his dad might, but he'd never gone like that on a Sunday. Michael didn't even know they did stuff on Sundays, but there were lots of people there. The entrance had shoes everywhere: some of them were paired, and others weren't, as if they'd been kicked around. It was always a mess like that. Even when he was a kid and they'd go for Eid, there were shoes everywhere.

His father went in ahead of him and sat in the front. It was a big room. There were wood pillars painted white and prayer rugs printed onto the carpet like they were tiles. The mihrab at the front had patterns on it and scriptures from the Quran. It made it look like it was this door going somewhere, but it went nowhere. It was all meant to look better than it was, but the mosque was in a converted bungalow that had been gutted. The inside looked like other mosques, but the outside was a bungalow. The front and back lawn had been paved over for parking. It wasn't anything special. It was in a subdivision with homes around it. They were supposed to move to a proper mosque, but they had never raised enough money for it so they had to stay there.

The imam was on the minbar, which looked like stairs that went nowhere, too. He was reading the Quran, acting like he was the only one there. Watching him like that, Michael thought how strange it was that someone could make a living reading a book and telling people what he thought about it. He was able to eat and pay his rent doing it. He wondered what made someone get into that line of work.

Michael went to the back of the room and sat against the wall just as this Iraqi kid in a gown got up at the front. He stood and put his right hand up until people stopped talking. It took a few seconds, but it didn't bug him to wait. He smiled; his eyes looked like he was half there.

When the room got quiet he started reciting verses from the Quran into a microphone. His voice went everywhere in the room. He couldn't have been more than ten years old. His face was soft brown; he was like a doll the way he opened and closed his eyes when he was singing the prayers.

Michael knew a lot of the verses he was reciting. He'd memorized them when he was a kid. His mom used to give him a dollar when he'd repeat them to family or friends. He'd usually say them really fast. The more he did, the more money he made, so he'd try to get through as many as he could. He would do a bunch back to back. Even today, he could repeat them—they were stuck in his head. He didn't know what any of it meant. He'd memorize them, but he didn't know what he was saying. He understood Arabic, like when his parents spoke the language, but the stuff in the Quran was different. It was an older Arabic that sounded like a different language.

Whenever the Iraqi kid finished a verse, he'd open his eyes and notice the crowd sitting there. Someone at the front would shout, "TAKBIR!" Everyone else would chant, "Allahu Akbar!"

"TAKBIR!"

"ALLAHU AKBAR!"

Michael's dad would sometimes be the first one shouting. When he did, he'd turn and check that Michael was still there. His dad smiled but looked sad. It was like he pitied him.

"TAKBIR!"

"ALLAHU AKBAR!"

"TAKBIR!"

"ALLAHU AKBAR!"

The imam got down from the stairs when the kid was done, and he turned to the people. He scanned the crowd—it was all part of the show. He smiled and waited another few seconds. When everyone was looking at him, he started talking about charity, or zakat.

Michael's phone went off in his pocket. It was a message from the guy on the app who he was talking to when he was on the bus. *What are you doing?* he wrote.

Just with my folks. U?

The guy sent a pic of himself driving. He wasn't looking at the camera, and was acting like he was paying attention to the road.

Michael sent a picture back of him sitting there. He didn't smile either. He stared at the imam who was still preaching to the crowd. He didn't know why he sent it, but he sent it.

The guy then followed up with a dick pic. It was hanging through the fly of his jeans and his balls were on the car seat. Michael put his phone away because he was afraid someone would see it. He looked around. There were two other guys leaning against the wall with him. With how they were sitting they wouldn't be able to see the screen of his phone. They weren't close enough to see it. When Michael felt sure, he got his phone out again.

Show me yours, the guy wrote.

I'm not at my parents' place, Michael said. *We're at the mall.*

Go to the washroom.

The imam was now hitting the air with his hand when he was talking. Everyone was listening—he had them in his control. No one noticed Michael leave the room, not even his dad.

The floor in the basement washroom had water everywhere from the foot baths. They'd never had towels down there. Even at other mosques there were never any—not even paper towels—and there was always water everywhere.

Michael tried not to step in the puddles, but his socks got soaked anyway. There was also a bunch of water on the floor in the bathroom stall he went into. There was nowhere to stand but right in it, so he stood in it.

He dropped his jeans and started playing with himself. It was hard to find anything good about it. All he could think was how he was standing in the mosque basement with soggy socks—he hated having wet feet. He could still hear the imam over the speakers—it wasn't helping.

Michael closed his eyes. He tried to think of something to get him going, but all he could hear was the sermon upstairs and feel his wet socks.

He grabbed his phone and pulled up the guy's dick pic. He thought of being there in the car with him, reaching over from the passenger side and sucking him off with his bare ass in the air. It was working, thinking of that. When he was hard enough, he took a pic of his dick. It filled the whole frame, making it look bigger than it was.

Fuck, the guy said after Michael sent it.

A minute later he wrote, *I'm Wyatt.*

I'm Mike.

When do I get to see you Mike?

Michael didn't answer right away. He waited a couple of minutes, then wrote, *I'm back in the city later today. I don't have anything planned.*

There's a pub in Cabbagetown—not far from my house.

o

Michael was fifteen minutes late meeting Wyatt. He took the streetcar because he thought it'd be quicker. He would've walked if he knew it'd take as long as it did. It felt like it was never going to come, and when it did it made so many stops, it would've been faster to walk.

Michael found him on the rooftop patio of the pub. His arms and legs were crossed and he didn't sit up when he noticed Michael standing there. He tilted his head and looked at Michael above his glasses. "Michael?"

"Sorry I'm late. I hate the TTC."

Wyatt kept staring. He wasn't smiling. Michael wondered if he was disappointed, seeing him in person: maybe he didn't think his photos matched, but he was sure his photos looked like how he looked.

He sat down—there was a full beer in front of him. "Is this for me?"

"If you want it."

"What is it?"

"Beer."

"What kind?"

"I can't remember. It's beer."

"Thanks." He lifted his glass. "Cheers."

Wyatt quietly lifted his too.

Michael mentioned the weather, how warm it was. He said he was glad summer was coming and started listing the things he wanted to do over the next few months: go to friends' cottages, camping, and spend some time at Hanlan's Point. Wyatt watched him but said nothing.

"Do you like going to Hanlan's?" Michael asked. "I go a lot, but I don't get naked."

"Never been."

"Really?"

"No interest." Wyatt picked his beer up and looked over Michael's shoulder.

"It's like getting out of the city without leaving," Michael said.

It seemed like Wyatt had stopped listening. Michael thought things would go better than this, but maybe Wyatt wasn't into how he looked in person.

Michael drank his beer and looked around too. He started counting in his head how long it was going to take for Wyatt to say something to him. He waited fifteen seconds, then thirty. After a minute, he stopped counting.

Then Wyatt said, "How's the family?"

"Good."

More silence.

"Just good?"

"It's always a bit of work."

"Why?"

"Lebanese parents can be extra."

Wyatt started looking over Michael's shoulder again—his mind went somewhere else, and Michael couldn't think of anything else to say. He figured it was a bad sign.

Wyatt looked back at him. "'Michael' doesn't sound Lebanese."

"My mom had a crush on Michael Caine. He reminded her of an uncle. He died in the war."

"Michael Caine." Wyatt smiled for the first time. It was a nice smile; it made it seem like his eyes changed from grey to blue.

"What about you?" Michael asked.

"What about me?"

"Are you from here?"

"I grew up on a farm outside of Dallas."

"I thought I heard an accent. So you're, like, from a 'farm' farm?"

"Yes. I'm from a 'farm' farm. There were chickens and cows."

"What was that like?"

"It was normal."

"I've always thought about living on a farm."

"It's a lot of work."

"Why's that?"

"Because it's a farm."

Silence again.

The conversation went like that for ten minutes, stop and go, and when the waiter passed, Wyatt asked for the bill. That stopped the talking altogether. Neither of them said anything until the cheque came. Michael's drink was still half full.

He reached for his wallet, but Wyatt grabbed the bill. "I'm paying."

"We can just go halves or whatever."

"I'm paying."

Michael left it; there was nothing worse than paying for a bad date anyway.

When they left the pub, Wyatt started walking east without saying anything. Michael's apartment was the other way, but he figured he couldn't go without thanking him for the drink.

When he caught up to him, Wyatt turned and smiled. "I guess you're coming home with me?"

Michael thought it was so stupid for him to say that. It was even more dumb that Michael said he would. Maybe he did it because it was dumb. The whole day was dumb, so why not keep it going? It was something to laugh about with Nathan after.

He followed Wyatt through Cabbagetown but he wasn't watching the street names or numbers along the way. He wasn't paying attention to anything. He was just laughing to himself because of how dumb the day was.

Wyatt's place was painted white and grey with black shutters on the windows. There were bright green shrubs sticking out from flower boxes under each window on both levels. When they got inside, Wyatt grabbed Michael and kissed him. Michael wasn't thinking how dumb the day was anymore—the kiss made him forget about all that.

When Wyatt told him to go upstairs, Michael didn't question it. He marched up the steps. "Turn right," Wyatt said, following behind. He led him to the bedroom past walls covered in art.

Michael took his shirt off, and Wyatt told him to keep going, to take his pants and underwear off too, so he did. Michael tried to kiss him again, but Wyatt grabbed his wrists, walked him to the bed, and pinned him to the mattress. If Michael wanted a kiss, he had to earn it. Michael pushed with everything in him until he was red in the face. Wyatt was stronger, but he tried the best he could. He started thrusting his hips, pumping the air to get Wyatt off balance. Michael had never been treated so roughly, but it made him feel something that he'd never felt before.

He kept trying to throw Wyatt off balance and got one hand free, but Wyatt grabbed it and pinned him down even harder. Michael pushed and pushed until he couldn't breathe. His eyes went red and his tongue got fat in his mouth—it was like he was going to choke on it.

He couldn't push anymore; his body dropped onto the bed. There was nothing he could do.

"It's okay, boy," Wyatt said, letting go. "We're going to have lots of fun."

Michael had never done anything like that before, where it was so rough, but it did something for him. His mind wasn't wandering, thinking about his family, or his dad taking him to the mosque. It was in that room and nowhere else.

When they were done fucking, Wyatt said he wanted to see him again. Michael knew that he just wanted to fuck around some more—that was it—but he started going over a couple of times a week. They didn't talk much when he was there. He'd stay an hour at most. Wyatt didn't need him there more than that. It was sex—that was it and Michael was fine with it. It was good sex. When they were at it, they'd start wrestling—it always got rough like that. Michael thought it was part-stupid, but he liked it too. He couldn't say why, but it did something for him.

He kept going there for weeks. Wyatt would call him over, they'd fool around and he'd leave. He'd never stay over and they'd never really talk.

Michael didn't tell Nathan about any of it. Sometimes he'd come home with bruises on his body because they were fighting so hard. He didn't mind them. He'd press on them after; he liked that no one knew about them but him and Wyatt. Even if he told Nathan, he thought he wouldn't get it. He didn't get it himself, but he liked it and tried not to think too much about why.

6

Wyatt told Michael to come by after nine. When he showed up, Wyatt gave him a hug at the door. It wasn't something he ever did. He hugged him and smiled—he didn't do that a lot either, and he kept his hand on Michael's back even after they were done hugging.

Wyatt asked about his day. His eyes got bigger.

They went upstairs and had sex, that didn't change. It was rough, except when they were close to being done, Wyatt told Michael to get on top of him.

"Hold my arms down and cum in my mouth, boy."

They never talked when they were fucking so it threw Michael off. "What?" he said. He was trying to catch his breath.

"Hold my arms and shoot your load down my throat."

Michael grabbed his arms, held them over his head, and took a seat on his chest. He was already close when he shoved his dick into his mouth, so it didn't take him much to cum. He only had to pump his hips four times.

Wyatt swallowed his load and called him a pig but said, "Good boy."

Michael fell sideways off Wyatt and onto the bed next to him.

"Good boy," Wyatt said again, turning over and smacking his stomach. He told Michael he was staying the night. He wasn't asking; he was telling. He never wanted him to stay before and Michael didn't normally like sleepovers either—he could never get to sleep with someone next to him—but with Wyatt he wanted to try.

He thought they'd watch TV or do something before bed, but Wyatt got up and went through the house turning all the lights off and made sure the front door was locked. Michael was still in bed waiting, not knowing what to do.

Wyatt came back to the room and turned the lights off in there too. He didn't say they were sleeping, but that's what they were doing. Michael got under the sheets when Wyatt did.

"Come here," Wyatt said. He grabbed Michael and put his arms around him. "You happy?"

"Yeah." Michael could hardly move with the way he was wrapped in Wyatt's arms.

"You sure?"

"Yeah."

He wasn't just saying it either. Wyatt felt good on him. He could sleep like that even though he couldn't move. He knew he could sleep: his eyes were heavy and his body felt tired. And he was falling asleep but then Wyatt said, "What is it that you want?"

Michael opened his eyes, but it was too dark to see anything.

"What do you mean?"

"You know what I mean." Silence. "Come on, Michael."

"Like, in life?"

"You know what I mean."

"There's a lot that I want."

"You want me to be your sexual mentor."

Michael tried to sit up but Wyatt held him down. "My mentor?"

"If that's what you want."

Michael almost started laughing—they never talked, and this was what they were talking about now? But he didn't laugh because it sounded like Wyatt was being serious.

"It isn't what you want?"

"I've never thought about it."

"You don't want it then?" Wyatt said.

"I don't know."

"Just forget it."

"No. I mean yes. I guess I want it."

"You guess?" Wyatt chuckled.

"What does it even mean?"

"I'll teach you things."

"Like what?"

"There are things you don't even know that you want. I can tell. Do you know how I know?"

"How?"

"I was like you."

More silence.

"Okay. It's what I want," Michael said.

"You sure?"

"Yeah."

"Does the idea make you happy?"

"It does," he said, and he thought he meant it even though he still didn't get it.

"Good." Wyatt pulled him in even closer. "Now, go to sleep, boy."

o

When Michael woke up in the morning, he could hear Wyatt in the shower. He didn't feel like showering there, so he got up and started putting his clothes on. He figured he'd walk home. It wasn't even six and he didn't have to get to work anytime soon; he'd walk and pick up breakfast on the way. But when Wyatt came out of the bathroom he said he had to be at work early and insisted on driving him back to his place.

There weren't a lot of people in the streets on the drive over. Michael felt even sleepier with the streets so quiet, but he had to stay awake to tell Wyatt how to get to his apartment.

When they got there, Wyatt turned the car off. "Are you happy?"

"I am, yeah."

"Good," Wyatt said. "I want you to be happy, but things are going to change." He said that they were going to meet twice a week. They'd do Tuesdays and Thursdays. Michael had to be there at eight on both nights. "If you're late I lock the door. You don't want to be late with me. Got it?"

"Okay."

"You're sure you want this?"

"Yeah."

"Why?"

Michael couldn't think why, so he said, "Because I do," and Wyatt was happy with that.

"I know you do. Do you know how I know?"

"How?

"Because we're the same."

Michael still didn't get it, but he was starting to like the idea of Wyatt as his mentor. He wondered if they were the same like he said; if that's why Wyatt was doing all this. Michael never felt the same as anyone, but he liked the thought of it.

Michael had to cancel his Thursdays with Nathan since they were still meeting every week. He told him he was doing a course for work that was going to last a while but asked if they could do Wednesdays. It wouldn't be forever, and Nathan said he didn't mind. He was still seeing the guy from before, the young one. He was fine with it so they changed their days to Wednesdays.

o

Wyatt messaged him a few hours before they were supposed to meet on that first Thursday with instructions. He said he was going to keep the front door unlocked and that Michael needed to come in, take his clothes off, and drink the glass of Scotch that would be left by the stairs. He told him again not to be late—if he was late he'd lock the door and he'd be sorry about it. Michael said he wouldn't be, that he shouldn't worry.

You'll be the one worrying if you're late, Wyatt said.

When he got to Wyatt's place, he opened the front door slowly, went in, and took everything off, even his socks. His body was buzzing, and it wasn't just because of the glass of Scotch that Wyatt had left by the door. Michael had been there so many times, but it looked different without Wyatt there greeting him at the door.

Wyatt had told him to go up to his room so he went up slowly, trying not to make any noise. He got to the top and he turned right. Wyatt wasn't in the bedroom, but there was a blindfold on the bed like he said there'd be. Michael put it on and got on his hands and knees. He closed his eyes. Even with the blindfold on, he shut them tight.

The first thing he felt was something whack his ass. It made a loud crack. He jumped—he didn't hear Wyatt come in—but it didn't hurt like how it sounded. Wyatt kept going at it, whacking him, making lots of noise. Michael didn't say anything since Wyatt had warned him not to. That was another rule. Don't be late, and no talking. He said if he started talking, he'd send him home.

After he was done whacking him, Wyatt made him suck his dick. He slapped his face a few times when he was doing it. They were proper slaps—he was seeing stars even though he had the blindfold on.

Wyatt finished him off by fucking him. It hurt at first because of how quickly Wyatt put his dick in him, but Michael closed his eyes until it started feeling good. The only sound was of Wyatt grunting and Michael grunting a bit too. Wyatt kept going until he came inside him, and then it got quiet.

They both lay there without making any noise. When Michael felt he could, he took the blindfold off and rolled over so his head was on Wyatt's belly. He almost fell asleep like that, but Wyatt said he had to go. He said only one sleepover a week and it wasn't tonight. Michael looked up at him like it was a joke, so Wyatt told him to leave again.

Michael went back downstairs and put his clothes on. They were all over the floor by the front door. Wyatt had followed him down; he was wearing a robe.

When Michael was dressed, he was going to leave without saying anything. He tried opening the front door, but Wyatt held it shut. "Kiss me," he said.

Michael gave him a quick kiss on the lips, but Wyatt said, "Do it like you mean it."

Michael kissed him properly.

"There are rules," Wyatt said. "You need to learn the rules— it's a part of it. Got it?"

"Yeah."

"If you want it to stop, we can stop. Is that what you want?"

"No."

"Then get out of here."

○

Each time Michael went over, it'd always start the same way: he'd take his clothes off, drink Scotch that Wyatt would leave out for him, and go upstairs. It got different from there. Sometimes he'd get tied up or flogged. Sometimes he'd blindfold him and sometimes he didn't. The start was the same, but the end was different each time.

Michael got this feeling in his stomach each time he went over, not knowing where things would lead. Maybe that was the point? It made him feel funny but it got him going too; it wasn't like stuff he had ever done before. It made him feel more alive, like he was finally waking up.

Each time, Wyatt pushed him further—he'd tie him up more or hit him harder, leaving marks that'd last days and make his bones ache. Michael always felt better after. He went home bruised, but he'd be buzzing for hours—it didn't make sense but it felt so good. He figured that's what Wyatt was showing him. The more he did it, the more he needed it.

There was one time Wyatt went so hard whacking him with a strap that Michael's back started bleeding. The whip cracked and knocked the wind out of him. He'd been on his hands and knees, but he dropped onto the bed. Wyatt was about to go at him again, but he must've seen that Michael was done. Wyatt dabbed the blood with his finger to show Michael. He started laughing. "It could've been worse," he said. "Next time it might be."

Michael tried to get himself up, but he couldn't. He didn't have anything left. He was tired and couldn't move. He could've slept like that. If he closed his eyes he would've. He'd already slept there one night that week, but he wasn't going to move.

He rolled on his side and stared up at the ceiling. His face got serious.

"Are you okay, boy?" Wyatt said.

Michael focused on the fan spinning over his head. When he blinked it looked like it was moving slower.

"Did you hear me?"

"I need to go to sleep."

"Then go to sleep."

Michael closed his eyes. He felt the sleep coming on heavy but before he slipped into it, he said, "You hurt me."

"You don't like it?"

"It hurts."

"Do you want to stop?"

Michael moaned and started falling asleep again.

"This isn't for everyone," Wyatt said. "My job is to find your limits."

"I know." Michael moaned again.

"Do you?"

Michael didn't say anything.

"All of this that we're doing—do you think it's for you?"

Michael opened his eyes. He couldn't see Wyatt's face from where he was. "Yeah."

"Of course it is."

Silence again.

"Why don't we do anything normal?" Michael said.

"What's normal?"

"We've never done dinner."

"No dinners. I'm your sexual mentor. We talked about this."

"Why?"

"No dinners."

"Okay, but why?" Michael whispered.

"Because."

"Because why?"

"Because I said so. Don't be stupid."

Michael closed his eyes. He cleared his throat. "So, it's just fucking?"

"Fuck you," Wyatt said. "It's more than that. You know it."

"Then what is it?"

Wyatt sat up so Michael could see him. He was squinting like he was studying Michael, acting very serious; he wasn't playing. Michael wasn't scared though; Wyatt was teaching him not to be scared.

"You want to do something 'normal'?" Wyatt said.

"I'm just asking."

"'I'm just asking,'" Wyatt repeated. "Tomorrow, we'll have drinks. No dinner though. Is that fuckin' normal?"

Michael smiled but didn't say anything.

"Is that what you want?"

"Yeah."

"Good." Wyatt kissed him on the head. "Now no more talking, or I'm going to make you go home."

7

Michael wore a blue button-down shirt to Wyatt's and put on cologne that smelled like mint. He picked up a bottle of wine that cost thirty bucks. He never paid that much, but he wanted something nice to bring so he asked the girl at the shop, and she told him it was a decent bottle.

When he got to Wyatt's, he didn't walk right in the way he usually did. He rang the bell—it didn't seem right to go in without being invited. When Wyatt opened the door, Michael tried to hand him the wine. "This is for you," he said, but he wouldn't take it.

"You didn't need to bring anything." He told him to close the door and went into the kitchen, leaving Michael standing there with the bottle.

Michael showed it to him again in the kitchen. "What do you want me to do with it?" Wyatt stared at him from above his glasses, but he said nothing. "Okay, I'll open it." Michael started going through the drawers, looking for a corkscrew. "Here it is," he said. "Where are the wine glasses?"

"Make yourself at home." Wyatt grabbed two glasses from the cupboard.

Michael talked about work. He'd never told him what he did for a living, so he started with that and listed off campaigns he'd worked on. He asked Wyatt if he'd seen any of them on TV.

"There are no commercials on Netflix," Wyatt said. "That's all I watch."

"Our stuff is online too."

"I don't know the ads you're talking about."

Michael opened the wine and poured himself a glass. "I wish I didn't have to work," he said. "I just want to travel. Go to Africa or Mongolia. Somewhere interesting."

Wyatt sat across from him on the kitchen island.

"A lot of people in Mongolia are nomads. Did you know that?"

"No, Michael. I didn't know that."

"It's true. I think some of them sleep in yurts that they move around. There are more horses there than people. That's what someone told me."

Michael tasted the wine, letting it sit in his mouth for a second before swallowing. "It's good wine."

"I wouldn't know. My glass is empty."

"Oh." He poured Wyatt some. "Sorry."

"No, problem, Michael."

"So?"

"So?"

"How was your week?"

"Good."

"Just good?"

"Yes."

"I don't even know what you do for work."

"You don't."

"What do you do?"

"I work."

Michael laughed. "What kind of work?"

"Restore things."

"What do you mean?"

"Redevelopment. Buildings."

"I don't get it."

Silence.

"We could be doing more important things right now," Wyatt said.

"You don't think this is important?"

"No."

"I'm enjoying myself."

"Good. I'm happy. I'm here to make you happy, Michael."

Wyatt smelled the wine before trying some but spit it back out after he took a taste. "You're trying to poison me," he said. He grabbed the bottle and poured it into the sink.

"What are you doing?"

"Get a bottle from down there." Wyatt pointed to the cupboard by Michael's feet. "Never bring anything again."

"I like this wine and the woman at the LCBO said it's a good one."

"Grab one now."

There were a bunch of bottles in the cupboard that were all the same, so Michael took one and tried to hand it to Wyatt.

"Don't give it to me. Open it."

Michael's face heated up because of how stupid he felt; he'd paid more for the bottle than he'd ever paid.

"You don't bring anything when you come here."

"You said that already."

"I mean it."

"Tell me what wine you like and I'll bring it."

"Just pour me some of that one." Wyatt was holding up his glass. "Put a little. Let me taste it."

Michael poured him a bit like at a restaurant. Wyatt swirled it around and smelled it twice before tasting it. He was acting like he had to think about it. Michael drank lots of wine, but he didn't know good wine from bad; he wasn't sure if he believed that good wine even existed.

"Excellent," Wyatt said. "Now pour yourself a glass, then finish filling the rest of mine. That's how you're supposed to do it."

Michael poured some for himself, then Wyatt. When he took a taste, he thought it'd be different from the other one, but he couldn't tell the two apart. Wyatt said it was from California; that they had the best wine in the world. He said America was the best at everything they did. It made Michael laugh—he thought Wyatt was joking.

"You think it's funny?" Wyatt said.

"People are people."

"What does that mean?"

"They can do good things no matter where they are."

"Tech. Media. Sports. Medicine—Canada doesn't even come close."

"I don't know if that's true."

"It's true."

"Then why are you here?"

"Don't worry about why I'm here," Wyatt said. "This is making you happy?" He said, shrugging.

"I'm having fun."

"Really?"

"Yeah."

"Why?"

"I'm learning more about you."

"Is that what you think?"

"The more I learn about someone, the more I like them."

"If you like what you learn."

"I like what I'm learning."

"Right."

"I think it makes the sex better if I know more about some-one."

"You don't like the sex we have?"

"I do, but I want to know who you are."

"Well, I've told you what I think about wine and America. You'd better cum twice as much next time." He lifted his glass and hit it against Michael's.

"Do you have a question for me?" Michael said.

"Yes, I do have a question. I'm glad you asked, Michael."

"Then ask."

"What are you curious to try?"

"What do you mean?"

"With sex."

"Shut up."

"You asked if I had a question. That's my question."

"Fine," he said. He had a mouthful of wine while he thought about the question. "I want to try handcuffs. The real ones, made of steel. The ones cops use."

"Stand up," Wyatt said.

"Why?"

"Stand up!" he shouted.

Michael jumped out of his chair and looked him in the eye to see if he was joking around, but he was acting serious. It scared him a bit to see Wyatt's mood change so quickly. Wyatt came around and twisted his arms behind his back. He held both wrists with one hand. "This is what you want?"

"What are you doing?"

"Is this what you want?"

"I guess."

"You guess?" Wyatt shoved him across the kitchen. Michael almost tripped over himself.

"What the fuck?"

"Take your clothes off."

"We're having drinks."

"Clothes off!"

Wyatt grabbed Michael's hand and put it on his dick. It was so hard it was pushing against his pants, stretching them. "That's what you do to me. Do you understand? Now take your clothes off. I'm not going to ask you again."

Michael pulled his jeans down. He was breathing heavy. He took his shirt and socks off, too. The vent from the A/C was blowing right on him, giving him goosebumps. He crossed his arms over his chest to keep himself warm.

"You better have those panties off when I get back down," Wyatt said. He ran out of the kitchen and up the stairs. Michael could hear his feet stomping the floor over his head.

Michael grabbed his underwear from the one side to get them off. He stepped out of them but was thinking how they were supposed to be having drinks. He was getting mad thinking about it, but his dick was hard too. When Wyatt came back down the stairs, Michael covered his crotch with both hands. He didn't want him to see that he was hard.

Wyatt dangled a pair of metal handcuffs on his finger. "This is what you want?"

Michael stared at them.

"I asked you a question. This isn't what you want?"

"Sure."

"Sure, what? You want to go home?"

"It's what I want."

"'It's what I want,'" Wyatt mimicked. "I hope you don't regret it."

He turned Michael around and pushed him up against the fridge with his face up against the stainless steel. Wyatt started cuffing his hands behind his back. He made them as tight as he could, digging into his bones. It felt like his wrists were ringing.

"Is it still what you want?"

"It hurts."

"That's not what I asked."

The pain from his wrist was shooting up his arm; he'd never felt anything like it before. "It's not as sexy as I thought it would be."

"You thought they'd be sexy?"

"Sexier than this."

"It's not, but at least you tried." Wyatt unlocked his right wrist. The ringing didn't go away, even when he took the handcuff off. It was like he couldn't get away from it.

"Did you hear me?" Wyatt asked.

"Yeah."

"Yeah?" Wyatt locked the free handcuff to his wrist so they were attached. "What do you want?"

"What do you mean?"

Wyatt threw his arm back, pulling Michael forward. He screamed—it felt like his wrist was being sliced and the pain from his back returned from being strapped yesterday.

"What do you want?"

"I don't know!"

Wyatt threw his arm back again.

"That hurts!"

He was sure he was bleeding, but when he checked his wrist, he wasn't.

"What do you want?"

"I don't know. I said that already."

"You don't know?"

Wyatt pulled him forward once, then twice. When he tugged at him a third time, Michael jumped at him and reached for his ankle. He was trying to take Wyatt down but missed his leg. Wyatt pulled him up.

"I said, that hurts!" Michael shouted.

"If you want to stop, we can stop. It hurts me too, but you don't see me crying like a bitch."

"I'm not a bitch."

148

"You're my bitch." His head was tilted forward when he laughed. "Or am I your bitch?"

Wyatt pulled at him and they kept going at it like that, wrestling in the kitchen. Michael was sweating all over, but he kept trying to take Wyatt down. Sweat was dripping from his hair, making the floor slippery.

His whole arm had gone numb from his shoulder to his fingertips. He couldn't feel it anymore, no matter how much Wyatt tugged at him. He was getting dizzy too—it felt like he was floating. His breathing was out of control, going faster, but it didn't stop him from chasing Wyatt's ankles. Even when everything started going black, making him sleepy, he didn't stop. He could never reach his ankles—they were always far away.

He didn't know how he got on the floor, but he was on the floor laid out in a puddle of his own sweat. He shut his eyes, but the room was spinning even with them shut.

He heard the handcuff come off. It's what woke him. He stared at the ceiling, but Wyatt whacked Michael's dick that was balancing over his body, standing up hard. "What's this?" he said.

Michael rubbed his wrist. It still felt like the handcuff was on even though he'd heard it come off.

"Get up," Wyatt said.

Silence.

"Get up. Get up, I said!" he whacked his dick again.

Michael had to shut his eyes to get himself onto his stomach. His hands slipped in the puddle of sweat and his chest smacked into the ground but he tried again and got himself up. He thought he was going to cry—it took so much out of him to get on his feet.

Wyatt got right in his face. "You need to call me 'sir' from now on," he said. "Did you hear me?" He snapped his fingers at his ear. Michael felt like he was going to fall over. "You need to call me 'sir.' No more 'Wyatt.' Got it?"

"Okay."

"Okay, what?"

"What?" He started seeing black again.

"Okay, sir."

"Okay, sir."

"Good boy." He smacked his head. "You're 'boy' now. That's it. Understand?"

Silence.

"Is this what you want? Be honest."

When Michael tried to answer, he started crying. He couldn't help himself. He felt embarrassed by it, but he couldn't stop. He didn't get why he was crying, but Wyatt wasn't surprised by it. It was like he was expecting it, the way he smiled. It's like that's what he was trying to do.

"Let it out, boy," he said. "It's okay." Wyatt put his arms around him and grabbed onto him tight. "Let it out. You're a good boy. This is what you're meant to be."

o

Michael woke up feeling like the day before didn't happen, but his body still ached when he tried to move, which was proof that it did. He lifted his head and could hear Wyatt showering. He tried to turn and look at the bathroom door, but it made the aching worse so he stopped. He looked down: his one wrist was bruised like it'd never been bruised before.

Wyatt came out a few minutes later, but Michael pretended to be asleep with the sheets over his head and eyes closed. Wyatt started whistling. He wasn't whistling a song Michael knew. It sounded like it was something he made up, but he wasn't being loud about it. Michael listened to him put his pants on too. He kept whistling, putting them on. He could hear the belt buckle tapping against itself. After that, he heard nothing. It was silent for five minutes—there was no noise, but then Wyatt smacked the bed. "Get up!" he said. He yanked the sheets off Michael. "It's six-thirty!"

Wyatt was wearing a blazer and dark jeans: everything looked brand new, like he didn't even wash his clothes after he bought them.

He smacked the side of the bed again. "Come on, move, boy!"

"Okay."

"Okay? Okay what?"

"What?"

"'Okay, sir.'"

"Okay, sir."

"Don't make me remind you again, boy. That's a warning."

"Okay, sir."

"Good boy."

When he crawled out of bed and stood up, Wyatt kissed him on his forehead, then looked him in the eye. "Get moving. I'm not going to be late because of you."

Michael got dressed and flattened his hair with his hand in front of the mirror. He noticed more bruises. It wasn't just on his wrist—they were all over his body. Not as bad as his wrist, but they were there.

"Boy?! Come on!" Wyatt shouted. He was downstairs now.

Michael came down and went out to the car. Wyatt came out a second later, wearing a hat Michael had never seen that was flat on top and made of wool. He couldn't tell if he liked it or not—it made him look like someone else. When he got in the car, he took it off and put it on the dashboard. He didn't say anything about it and Michael didn't say anything either.

Before he started driving, Wyatt unbuttoned his cuff and showed Michael his wrist. It was bruised too. "We're twins," he said, laughing to himself. He reached over and squeezed Michael's hand. Their bruised wrists were side by side. It made Michael feel better about it, that they were the same. Wyatt didn't let go of his hand. Even when he started driving, they kept holding hands, and it made Michael like the bruising more and more. He didn't let go until they got to Michael's building.

"Give me a kiss, boy," Wyatt said. They'd never done that in public. There was a guy across the street walking his dog. He was looking over at them—he was from Michael's building. He knew him from the elevator. Wyatt would've seen him walking his dog, but he didn't care. Michael reached over and kissed him, falling on the console between them. The guy with the dog was still watching; Michael tried to ignore him.

"You're a good boy," Wyatt whispered. "I'm really proud of you."

"Thank you, sir," Michael said, sitting back down in his seat. His body hurt but it made him feel good knowing it was because of Wyatt, and that Wyatt was hurting because of him.

"I know you don't understand everything right now," Wyatt said. His grey eyes were all Michael could see. "You will though. Do you trust me?"

"I do . . . sir."

"I know you do. Do you know how I know? Because we're the same." He held up his bruised wrist to show Michael again. "Do you understand?"

"Yes, sir," he said.

"Do you know what else?"

"What, sir?"

"You're ready for more, but I need dedication. You have to really want this."

"Okay."

"Do you want this?"

Michael nodded.

"I need you to say it."

"I want this . . . sir."

Wyatt said they were going to start doing three days a week now, not two, and Michael wouldn't know the day until an hour before. He had to be ready whenever Wyatt needed him and said he was going to need him a lot. Michael didn't know what it was like to have someone need him like that, but it made him feel like he mattered.

"It could be the evening and weekends—that's the dedication I need. If you're not serious, tell me now."

"I'm serious."

"You're serious, what?"

"I'm serious, sir."

"You're lucky, do you know that? Do you know why?"

"Why, sir?"

"You have your whole life ahead of you."

o

That week Wyatt went out and bought him a leather mask that had holes for the eyes and mouth. There was another piece that snapped on to cover the eyes if he wanted to cover them. He wrote Michael's name on the inside tag with a marker and said that if Michael was in the house, he had to put it on. He left it by the umbrellas near the front door so it was the first thing Michael did when he came in. Put the mask on and take his clothes off— those were the new rules. If Michael was going to be there, Wyatt wanted to see all of his body.

Wyatt tied him up in rope the first time he wore the mask. It made him sweat; not just his head but his whole body because it was so hot. Michael thought it'd be hard to breathe in it too, but it wasn't bad, and when he started to get tied up he forgot about how hot it was to wear.

Wyatt went easy the first time with the rope. It was tight enough that Michael couldn't move, but it didn't hurt. Each time after that though Wyatt would push it even more. He'd either hog-tie him or get him on the bed, face down, ass in the air, with his wrists tied to his ankles. Wyatt would fuck him like that, all tangled up. He'd get the rope so tight it started burning and he would bruise for days.

He'd always get Michael crying. Even if he didn't want to cry, he'd cry. Letting go the way Wyatt got him to made it so if he felt tears coming, he couldn't stop them—he'd start balling. It was like those tears had been building up for years and Wyatt was the only one who knew how to get them out of him. Michael would be crying so hard he'd start heaving—he couldn't stop, but Wyatt never made him feel dumb for it. It was the opposite; it was like Wyatt needed them—as much as he wanted to hurt Michael, he wanted to heal him. When Michael really got going, Wyatt would take the mask off and kiss him so that they'd both be eating the tears.

After he was done with his cries, he felt lighter. Any pains he had were gone. Even if Wyatt made him bleed, it didn't bug him. When he went home the next day, he still felt like he only weighed ten pounds and would smile when the raw welts rubbed against his clothes.

The deeper Wyatt took him, the more he wanted. He didn't care if his whole body was bruised and bleeding, he wanted more. It was all he could think about when he wasn't with Wyatt. He'd go to work, he'd go to the gym, sometimes see Nathan, but he was always thinking of when he'd see Wyatt again.

Wyatt couldn't control himself either. As much as Michael got something from it, it was like Wyatt got something too. He'd lose himself to the violence, going on his own trip—his eyes would turn white and get wild; he'd sweat from everywhere and even with deodorant on Michael could smell his odour.

It got so heavy they were doing four or five days a week. Once they did six days, but Michael still needed more. He told him that, but Wyatt said they needed a break because his body got so beat up. He was travelling for work anyway, going to British Columbia for a week—he said he was proud of him, but Michael needed to rest and he'd see him when he returned.

Wyatt left and one week turned to two, then three. He was only supposed to go to Vancouver, but there were problems elsewhere, so they sent him to the interior, to these small towns. No matter where he went though, they texted every day in the morning and at night. Sometimes they'd text in the daytime too.

Wyatt would send him pictures of himself wherever he was. He'd take them like someone else took them: he'd never be smiling or looking at the camera, and he'd try to get something in the background to show where he was. He'd write *THE BAR*, or *RENTAL CAR*, or whatever it was.

Wyatt was gone so long all the welts on Michael's body healed and his skin went back to normal. It didn't feel right to have nothing on him, and it made him miss Wyatt more. He told him that: he had nothing left and he needed him to get back so he could mark him up some more, but Wyatt said they were going to try something different when he returned because Michael was ready. When Michael asked what it was, he wouldn't say, except that he was ready.

"Do you think you have it in you, boy?" Wyatt said.

"Yes, sir."

"Do you trust me?"

"Of course."

"This is what you're meant to be. Do you understand?"

"I do, sir."

"You know I'm proud of you, right?"

Michael smiled. "I know, sir."

"Don't forget that, boy. Anyone can fantasize, but only real men act. Do you understand?"

Michael had to think about it. "Yes, sir," he said, even though he had to keep thinking. Maybe he was talking about them and the stuff they were doing, but he wasn't sure.

"We can't have you marked up for what comes next."

°

The afternoon Wyatt got back, he said needed to see Michael. They didn't wait until eight like most times. Wyatt told him to come over as soon as he could, so Michael finished work and walked over right from there. It was just after six and the sun was still out. It felt earlier than it was. He had a jacket but held it in his hand because it was so hot out.

His body was buzzing, going across the downtown through the crowds and up to the village. He smiled the whole way; the sun was making him giddy. He was walking faster than he'd normally walk.

When he got to Wyatt's, he opened the front door without knocking. Wyatt was in the living room, sitting on the sofa facing the front door. He looked up from his magazine, over his glasses. Michael missed his grey eyes the most—that was his favourite part of him.

"Hi," Michael said.

"I fuckin' missed you, boy."

Michael smiled more. He felt goofy for how he was smiling.

He started taking his clothes like he was supposed to but Wyatt told him to stop. He asked him to sit.

"What about the hood?"

"Not today, boy. I need to see your face."

Silence.

"Okay, sir."

"Come sit down." He patted the cushion next to him. Wyatt put his hand on his leg and started kissing him. He held the back of his neck and put his tongue in his mouth. It went in so deep it felt like he was trying to lick his belly.

Wyatt pulled him away. His eyes turned white. "I missed you," he said. "I should bring you with me next time. Keep you in the room for when I need you."

"Would you need me a lot, sir?"

"Yes, boy."

Michael's smile felt like it was going to stretch off his face.

"You'd like that, wouldn't you, boy?"

"Yes, sir."

"You want to be my gimp, waiting for me to fuck you?"

"Yes, sir."

"I know you would." He let go of his leg and lifted his empty glass. "Now go get me more Scotch. Get yourself one too, boy."

Michael took his glass and went to the kitchen. There was a bottle on the counter so he poured Wyatt some and grabbed a glass for himself.

When he came back, Wyatt was grinning. "Cheers," he said, taking his glass.

"Cheers."

Michael sat again and Wyatt put his hand down the front of Michael's pants. He started telling him about the trip, things Michael already knew because they'd been texting the whole time. Wyatt didn't make a big deal of having his hand in his pants, and Michael acted like it was nothing too even though he was starting to get hard.

Michael didn't put his glass down. He kept drinking the Scotch. It didn't take long for it to hit him because he hadn't eaten anything since breakfast.

Wyatt kept talking like he didn't notice Michael's dick growing in his hand. There was no way he didn't notice, but that's how he was acting.

Wyatt started talking about a "boy" he saw when he was in Vancouver. It was someone he'd known for years. Michael didn't understand that part. He kept holding his glass. He took another sip, but he wasn't sure whether he'd heard right. "Who?" Michael said.

"He's another one of my boys. He's a gimp though, right? That's all he wants to be."

Wyatt took his hand out from Michael's pants, maybe because he felt Michael getting soft. He stopped looking at Michael too—he looked at the kitchen, then his glass. He finished the rest of his Scotch and grabbed Michael's glass from his hand. He downed Michael's too and said, "More?" but he still wouldn't look at him.

"Sure."

"Now I'm your gimp." Wyatt laughed and went to the kitchen, but he kept talking. He said when he was in Vancouver, this "boy" stayed in his hotel room locked up in a sleep sack. He was locked up even when Wyatt wasn't there. He only unlocked him when he needed to use him, but if he wasn't using him he was in a sleep sack blindfolded and muzzled, no breaks. Michael's body got stiff. When Wyatt came back with his drink, it was hard for him to take the glass, but he made himself do it and tried to act normal.

Wyatt sat down but he didn't put his hand down his pants again. He didn't touch him. "Cheers," he said.

"Cheers."

Michael was starting to get it. Everything Wyatt was saying was catching up in his head. He didn't get the sleep sack part—if the guy was locked up, when did he eat or drink? He'd have to eat or drink. He didn't get that part, but he got the other stuff.

Wyatt was acting differently—that was making Michael mad too—he still wasn't touching him. He was talking about work some more and drinking his drink. He never talked about his work that much. It was the sort of talk Wyatt hated and he wouldn't let Michael talk like that.

He felt stupid for thinking he had Wyatt to himself. And from how Wyatt was talking, it wasn't just the gimp either. If he was one of his boys, it meant there were others, more than him and the gimp. *And what the fuck is a gimp?* Michael thought. He knew there was a gimp in *Pulp Fiction*; it sounded like maybe it was the same thing as the movie.

He was starting to sweat because of how mad he was getting. When Wyatt wasn't looking, he wiped it.

Wyatt kept talking about stuff, but Michael couldn't focus on what he was saying. He had to balance the glass on his thigh so it wouldn't slip from his hand. He started thinking about all the people Wyatt was with when they weren't together. He was thinking it so hard the glass could slip if he wasn't careful.

"Are you okay, boy?" Wyatt said.

Michael lifted his glass and took a sip. "I'm fine."

"You're fine, what?"

"I'm fine, sir."

"Good boy." He put his hand down the front of his pants again, but Michael's dick was shrivelled. Wyatt laughed. "What happened?"

"Do you want another drink, sir?" Michael said, throwing the rest of his Scotch back.

"One more, but we can't have you getting drunk. I have plans for you tonight."

"What plans, sir?"

"You'll see."

"Okay, sir."

Michael went to the kitchen. He took two big gulps of Scotch right from the bottle before pouring their drinks. It almost made him throw up, having that much at once. It tasted good sipping it, but having a mouthful wasn't the same. He had to stop himself from coughing; he closed his eyes and wiped his mouth. When he was normal again, he brought their drinks out.

"Are you sure you're okay, boy?"

"Yeah, I'm fine."

"Are you still happy to see me?"

He was feeling dizzy. He couldn't look at him. He was looking at his feet. "Yes, sir."

"I'm happy to see you."

"I know."

Wyatt put his hand on his thigh. He made Michael look at him. "Do you believe me?"

He couldn't tell if Wyatt knew what was going on in his head.

"You're my favourite boy," he said. "Don't forget that. Do you understand?"

"I think so, sir."

"You'll see there's no reason to be jealous. Jealousy is for common people, and you're not common. Do you know how I know?"

"How?"

"Because we're the same, and I'm not fuckin' common either. And I need my number one boy to be strong. Are you strong?"

"Yes, sir."

"Say it."

"Say what?"

"That you're strong, boy. Don't be stupid."

"I'm strong."

"Say it again."

"I'm strong."

"I fuckin' missed you, boy." Wyatt kissed him again but this time he got on top of him. His tongue was down his throat, and his hands shoved in his pants. "You're strong," he said between kisses.

Michael got hard so Wyatt pulled his pants down a bit with one hand because he said he wanted to see it. He kept telling him he's strong and started stroking him, but when he got close to cumming, he stopped.

"Take all your clothes off," he said. Wyatt didn't move from the sofa; he was leaning across the cushions, using his elbow to keep his body up. He watched Michael stand and pull his pants down the rest of the way. Michael took his shirt and socks off too. Wyatt looked at his body. He wasn't smiling, he wasn't doing anything, he was just looking.

"Go upstairs, boy. I have something on the bed. Put it on and wait for me."

"Yes, sir."

Wyatt was right behind him when he went up the stairs. He didn't make him wait like he said he was going to.

There was a pair of jeans on the bed. That was it, nothing else. Michael picked them up—they were Abercrombie—he never wore that stuff. Even when he was younger, he didn't like it and he'd never seen Wyatt wear it either. He always noticed the clothes he wore, and sometimes he went through his closet. All he had were Wrangler or Levi's. The ones on the bed must've been new because he'd never seen them.

"Put them on, boy," Wyatt said.

"They're just jeans."

"Put them on."

They were too big for him. They fell to his hips and got caught under his heels, but Wyatt was smiling now.

"Turn around," he said. "I want to see your ass."

Michael did as he was told but had to hold the waist up so they wouldn't fall.

"Boy, are you ready to try something different?"

"What is it?"

"Are you ready, yes or no?"

"Yes, sir," Michael said slowly.

"When the doorbell rings downstairs, I want you to open it. There will be a guy there; he's about your age. Bring him up to me. Do you think you can do that, boy?"

"Who are they?"

"Who are they, what?"

"No, who are they?"

"He's a nobody. Calm down, boy. Don't worry. I know that look—don't worry. I found him online, but he's nothing."

"Why is he here?"

"He's not here. He's coming."

"You know what I mean."

Silence.

"You know why."

"Like a threesome?"

"It's not just a threesome. Don't be stupid. Do you trust what I'm teaching you, boy?"

Trust wasn't what he was feeling. There were a lot of things he was feeling, but that wasn't it. He didn't get it; why bring someone over? That's what he was thinking.

"I asked you a question, boy."

"I just want to do the stuff we normally do."

"So you don't trust me?"

"I don't understand."

"What don't you understand, boy?"

"I just want to do what we normally do."

"I know, boy, but my job is to teach you so you have to trust me—I'm your mentor. I'm not your boyfriend. I teach you but if you don't trust me, we have nothing, boy. Understand?"

Michael rolled his eyes. "Yes, sir."

"I trust you with my life, but if you don't trust me, you should leave. You know where the door is."

Michael didn't say anything because he was trying to think. He was feeling lots of things, but he didn't want to leave.

"If you're not going to trust me boy, you can go."

"Fine, I trust you."

"Fine?"

"I trust you."

"I can't hear you. Louder."

"I trust you."

"I trust you, what?"

"I trust you, sir."

Wyatt went up to him and pushed his forehead against Michael's. He grabbed the back of his neck and looked him in the eye. "I trust you with my life. Don't fuckin' forget that, boy."

"I won't, sir."

"You won't, that's right." Wyatt got on the bed and leaned against the headboard. "Are you still happy to see me?"

"Yes, sir."

"You still miss me as much as you missed me before?"

"I do, sir."

"Good. So when the guy comes, you bring him up to me, but I want you to take his shirt off before he gets here. Got it, boy?"

"When is he going to be here?"

"He'll be here when he's here. Now go get me a glass of Scotch. Get yourself one too. You need to relax."

When Michael went down the stairs, he had to be careful not to trip on the heels of the jeans. He bunched them up around his knees so he could walk properly.

Both their glasses were still on the coffee table, but he couldn't tell whose was whose. There was a bit left in both so he finished it all and went to the kitchen to fill them up again. That's when the doorbell rang.

His body froze. He had the two glasses in his hand and was mid-step, but his left foot was hanging over the floor. He stayed like that for two, maybe three, seconds then put the glasses on the counter. "Wyatt, do I get that?!" he shouted. "Wyatt?!"

The doorbell rang again.

"Answer it!" Wyatt shouted back. He didn't sound happy.

Michael opened the door. There was this guy looking back at him, smiling. He had big lips—it was the first thing he noticed. It was like they could be taken off and put back on like Mr. Potato Head's lips. He was tall too, a couple of inches bigger than Michael but he looked much younger. He was probably twenty-one. Even for Michael he was young; he was the sort of guy Nathan would be into. It seemed like Wyatt liked young ones too. The guy had big shoulders, a big chest, but his face was like a baby's.

"You look like your photos," the guy said as Michael let him in.

"Do you want a drink?"

"No. Thank you."

Michael thought it'd be good to kiss him before going up, so that's what he did. He didn't tell him he was going to kiss him, he just kissed him and the guy liked it—he kissed him back. His lips felt as big as they looked.

Michael took the guy's shirt off like Wyatt told him to and said that he had to follow him upstairs.

Wyatt was sitting in bed, reading a paper when they came up. He acted surprised seeing them, like he was pretending that he didn't know they were coming. "You're a big guy, aren't you?" Wyatt said. He got out of bed and rubbed the guy's chest. "Sexy too."

The two of them started kissing. Wyatt was moaning too—he never moaned like that so it sounded weird, but everything about him today was different.

They pulled each other's clothes off while they were kissing until they were naked and their dicks were touching. None of it was doing anything for Michael so he got on his knees between them, trying to get into it. He went for Wyatt's dick and started sucking. Then he went over to the other guy's dick, but it was like his lips: the head of it was puffy and he didn't like it. He was about to go back to Wyatt's, but the two walked over to the bed and left Michael alone on his knees, in the middle of the room.

They got on the bed in a way so they could suck each other's dicks in a sixty-nine position. Michael crawled over and tried to join but he couldn't because of how they were curled into each other. All he could do was watch, so he sat back on the other side of the bed. He figured that if they noticed him doing nothing, they'd stop, but that's not what happened. Wyatt started fucking the guy right there, but he couldn't look at Michael while he was doing it. He was smiling and getting sweaty, but he couldn't look Michael in the eye. Wyatt kept going at him until it seemed like he was about to cum. He stopped himself and pulled out.

"Roll over," he told the guy, who rolled and started sucking Wyatt's dick like it was automatic. He elbowed Michael to get a good angle of it; he made Wyatt cum quick. He finished with a long huff like a horse would make.

The guy sat up and opened his mouth wide to show Wyatt that he'd swallowed it all but kept jerking himself and licking his lips. His whole body was flexing.

"I'm going to cum," he finally said.

"Then cum," Wyatt said.

He looked at Michael. "Will you eat it?"

"What?" Michael said.

"Do you want my cum?"

"No."

The guy ended up cumming off the side of the bed.

Wyatt opened his eyes. He seemed surprised to see Michael still there, but he told him to lie down next to him. He invited the third to lie down too, on the other side. He tried to put his arms around both, but Michael shrugged him off.

"He's mad," Wyatt said. "He didn't enjoy himself."

"I'm fine."

"Oh no!" Wyatt laughed. "He is mad."

"Fuck off!"

"Whoa, Michael. Michael? I'm joking. I'm having fun with you."

"This isn't fun."

Silence.

"I should go," the other guy said.

"You sure?" Wyatt was still looking at Michael. "He doesn't mean it."

"I need to meet a friend. I'm late."

The guy got up and started putting his clothes on. Michael had to look at the wall because it was taking so long, and it didn't feel right to be looking because they hadn't been fooling around except when they kissed at the front door.

"I'll walk you out," Michael said when he was all dressed. He went ahead of him, down the stairs. When Michael was letting him out the door, he smiled but couldn't look any higher than his chin.

"Maybe I'll see you again," the guy said.

"Maybe." He closed the door on him.

"You didn't like that." Wyatt was behind him, standing at the top of the stairs.

"Did you like it?"

"I didn't mind."

Michael still had his back to Wyatt with his hand on the door-knob. "I know."

"What does that mean?"

"I should go home."

"I thought you were staying tonight."

"I need to go home."

"I want you to stay," Wyatt said.

"Why?" Michael turned around and looked up at him.

"Because I missed you."

"I think you're a sadist."

"I'm not a sadist."

"You probably like seeing me like this."

"I'm not a sadist," Wyatt repeated and walked down two steps.

"You told me that you're a sadist, and now you're not?"

"I didn't say that."

"You don't even know what you are."

"I don't know what *I* am?"

"You guys were just having sex without me."

Wyatt chuckled and sat down on the step he'd been standing on. "What did you want me to do?"

"Stop."

"Oh, come on."

"So, I should just sit there and watch?"

"That's what you did."

"You're an asshole." Michael started laughing. "This is so stupid. Is this real?"

"You could've grabbed a beer."

"What do you mean?"

"If you weren't having fun you could've grabbed a beer."

Michael squinted and shook his head. "Are you being serious?"

"I've done that before."

"In the middle of sex?"

"You weren't having sex."

"I need to go home."

166

"I want you to stay."

When Michael went up the stairs, Wyatt got up and tried to grab him, but he wouldn't let him. He went to the room and started putting his clothes on.

"What was I supposed to learn today, mentor?" Michael said. "What was the lesson?"

Wyatt shrugged. "To relax and have fun."

"I guess you're a shitty teacher."

"I didn't even like the guy."

"It looked like you liked him."

"He knows how to give a blowjob. So what? It could've been anyone." Silence. "Stay. Please. Boy? It was just sex. That was the lesson. Sex can mean nothing. Come on. Stay."

"I need to leave and clear my head."

"Clear your head and come back."

Wyatt walked him down to the front. His eyes were teary and he didn't stop smiling, but he seemed nervous. Michael had never seen him like that.

"Are you coming back?" he said.

"I'm going home."

"That's fine. Go home, boy. Will you call me? Actually, don't answer that. Just call me."

Michael went out and shut the door behind him. He walked down the street and started thinking how Wyatt would say anything to get what he wanted, how everything about being a mentor and trying to teach him things was bullshit. He felt stupid for believing any of it.

On his way home, he replayed the whole evening in his head: everything from having the Scotch together, to the third showing up at the door, and them having sex in front of him pretending he wasn't there. He thought about the guy's fat lips, his dick that was like his lips, and the way he made Wyatt cum. And once he replayed the whole night in his head, he let it play all over again.

167

When he got home, he poured himself wine and tried to watch TV, but he was so far in his head, he couldn't focus on anything happening in front of him. He kept replaying the night, over and over. Even when he tried to go to sleep and shut his eyes, it's what he saw: Wyatt's face, the guy's lips, everything. It made him hate Wyatt more when he couldn't sleep. He kept turning in bed, and it felt like he was going crazy because he couldn't get the thoughts to stop.

He didn't get to sleep until close to five, but his alarm went off at six-thirty. He kept hitting snooze until seven, but he'd been late for work once this week, and his boss made a big deal of it. He got up, but before showering, he checked his phone. He got a rush seeing three messages from Wyatt because he'd always get excited seeing messages from him—it's how his brain worked. It even made him smile, but he didn't check them. He deleted the messages without reading them.

He got to work on time and was able to pick up a fried egg sandwich and coffee on the way. He sat at his desk checking emails and drinking his coffee, trying to keep himself awake. He was feeling like he could throw up because of how tired he was. He took small bites of his sandwich. It helped but he only ate more when he started feeling sick again.

Michael's desk was on the fifth floor of a high-rise. The art department took the whole floor. It was open concept—there were a bunch of cubicles with low walls all the way down and across, and glass windows past them looking onto another building. Nobody had offices, not even managers. They just had bigger cubicles with an extra desk, ledge, or cabinet. The better the job title, the bigger the desk.

June came in ten minutes after he did. She was a senior project manager who sat across from him in the same sized-desk. She cradled her stomach because of how pregnant she was. It was like she was going to burst, and the only way to stop it was with her hands.

"Hey hun," she said, sitting down.

"Morning."

She turned her computer on and stared out the window as she waited for it to get going. Michael was looking at her while she was waiting, but she didn't notice. She was playing with her blond hair, twirling it around with her finger. She had most of her hair tied up in a bun and was in this white dress with pink flowers all over it. Michael wasn't staring for any reason. He was tired, but he got to thinking how normal she was—how normal everyone at the office was. He liked her; they'd go for lunch together sometimes and usually complained about the same people, but it was all they had in common even though they acted like friends. She was newly married and had just moved into their first home with her second kid on the way.

She turned to Michael so they were looking at each other. "Come get a coffee with me."

He had hardly drank the one he had but was too tired to start working, so he said he'd go.

On the elevator down, she started telling him how she'd watched *Beetlejuice* with her kid last night and asked if Michael had seen it. He said he had when he was a boy but didn't remember much from it. She said that when they were at the table for breakfast this morning, her kid started singing this song from it. He was only five. She asked if he remembered the song, and she sang it for him in a weird voice: "Daylight come and me wan' go home. Daylight come, and me wan' go home."

"No, I don't know it," he said. "I saw the movie a long time ago."

When they got out of the elevator, she said that he looked tired.

He laughed. "Thanks. I am tired," he said. "I had trouble sleeping."

"I hate that. Everything okay?"

"I guess."

"Boy problems?"

"I guess so."

"Steven?" she said.

"Yeah."

He'd told her about Wyatt before but he never used his real name. He said his name was Steven because he'd never known anyone named Wyatt and worried that maybe she knew him. He didn't mention that he was almost double his age. He didn't think she'd get it—she was too normal.

He didn't tell her about him because he thought they were close friends—they weren't. They sat close together, and they'd get talking, that was it. It was the only reason why he mentioned any of it.

"What happened?" she said as they got in the coffee line. "And I'm buying you a coffee so put your money away."

"We had a fight."

"What about?"

He wanted to tell her; he knew he'd feel better if he said something, but he didn't think she'd get it.

"It was about stupid stuff," he said.

"We all have those. Me and Bry argue about laundry or dishes all the time. You learn that those things don't matter."

"Yeah, you're right."

"You don't want to be dating forever though. Do you like him?"

"Not right now."

"Why, what did he do?" She smiled. "Tell me."

He didn't want to talk about it anymore and wanted her to stop asking; he knew she'd be mad if he didn't say, but he was feeling too tired to make something up so he just said, "It was stupid stuff" again.

She sighed and rolled her eyes. "Whatever." It bugged her that he wouldn't say, like he knew it would. She started singing the song from *Beetlejuice* again quietly, but halfway through the first verse, she stopped and said, "You're so hopeless, but I love you anyway."

When his mom found out he was gay, she'd told him that he was a faggot and he'd never have a normal life, but he didn't want that anyway. Maybe he was hopeless, but he'd rather that than trying to be normal the way June was normal. He'd rather live the life he was living instead of the life he was supposed to live because that's what everyone else was doing.

○

Michael lay low the whole day, answering emails that needed answering and going to a couple of meetings, but he didn't do more than he needed to. He put in the day's work and drank lots of coffee to get him through.

He decided to walk home instead of taking the subway. He wasn't feeling as tired as he was before, and he grabbed another coffee on the way, hoping he'd get a second wind. He started wondering what Wyatt was going to get up to tonight. They were supposed to get together again, and he thought it'd be funny if he just showed up, ringing his doorbell and acting like nothing was wrong; coming in and taking his clothes off—he thought it'd fuck with Wyatt's head. He wasn't going to do it, but it made him laugh, thinking about it.

When Michael was halfway home, Nathan sent a message, asking what he was doing and if he felt like going to a patio on Church. He texted him right back, saying he was up for it. He told him he was walking home from work and could go there instead, so they planned to meet in half an hour.

Michael got there first and picked a seat that looked onto Church. It didn't take Nathan long to join him, but when he got there, he stood on the other side of the patio and waited for Michael to notice. It made Michael jump, seeing someone standing so close, staring at him, but when he saw who it was, he got up and hugged him over the rail. They never hugged like that. He kissed him on the cheek too, and Nathan noticed, and said, "What's this for?"

"Just happy to see you," Michael said.

Michael had already ordered them a pitcher of beer and started pouring Nathan a glass when he sat down. He got a Keith's even though he didn't like the taste of it. It was too sweet. He told him, "I got Keith's, your favourite," and handed him the glass. "Cheers," Michael said.

"You're too funny." Nathan clinked his glass.

"Why?"

"Because you are."

He felt good seeing Nathan. He was more himself with him there, in touch with a part of himself that he'd started to forget around Wyatt.

"How's the course going?" Nathan said.

He'd almost forgotten that he'd lied about a work course when he started seeing Wyatt more often.

"It's boring," he said. "But it's done now."

"I thought it was a full semester course."

"It's just training."

Michael asked about his boyfriend, Tyler, to change the subject, and they talked about that a bit. Nathan said things were going good, really good. Michael could tell it was making Nathan happy talking about him, and seeing him like that made Michael happy for him. Nathan told him they were going on their first trip together, to Barcelona. They were doing a couple of days in Sitges too, and he asked if Michael had ever been there. He hadn't, so Nathan told him about it—it wasn't far from Barcelona by train, no more than two hours, and he said it was really gay, like Provincetown but Spanish.

Seeing Nathan get excited made him more handsome to Michael. His face was relaxed, more than he'd ever seen. He was happy all over—he could even hear it in his voice, the way he was talking about Barcelona, getting excited about it. "It'll be my second time going," he said. "It's my favourite place."

"I didn't know that," Michael said, but the way he said it, it was like it bugged him, not knowing. "I should've known that."

"I think I told you."

"I don't remember."

"I love it there."

"I should've remembered."

Nathan started listing all the things they were going to do in Barcelona. Michael was interested, but he started feeling these new feelings. He was trying to smile, but it wasn't sitting right on his face.

He was happy to see Nathan. If he wasn't there, he didn't know what he would've done. He needed him there, but there was something that wasn't feeling right, and he didn't know where it was coming from. Michael was still trying to smile, but any time he pushed his cheeks up, it felt like he'd start crying. He didn't get it. Nathan was excited, and Michael didn't want to cry, but he had to stop trying to smile because it'd ruin the mood if he cried and he didn't want to ruin anything.

He stared at Nathan and tried to nod to show he was interested in what he was saying, because he was, even if something wasn't feeling right.

Nathan was now telling him about the bars in Sitges and one of the naked beaches there. He normally wouldn't go naked, but in Spain he doesn't mind doing it. When everyone does it, he's okay with it. Michael tried to laugh because he wanted to show he was listening, but even the idea of laughing made him feel like he could cry.

When Nathan stopped talking about Spain, Michael tried to think of something to say. Nathan had been saying so much, he felt he had to say something back, but he couldn't think of anything, so he stayed quiet and Nathan was quiet too. He was still smiling, but when he noticed Michael wasn't he stopped.

"There's something wrong," he said. "What's wrong?"

"There's nothing wrong," Michael said, but it made his eyes water, talking again.

"I know when there's something wrong. Is it your family? Did something happen?"

"It's not my family."

"Then what is it?"

"There's someone," he said.

"What do you mean 'someone'?"

"There's a guy. We weren't dating. That's why I didn't say any-thing, but I was seeing this guy for a bit."

Nathan still didn't get it, so Michael told him about Wyatt, starting from when they'd first met—how they got together on Father's Day, and he told him about some of the stuff they got up to in bed. Michael wasn't thinking about what he was saying: words were coming out and he wasn't trying to stop them. He told him everything right up to the threesome yesterday. He even mentioned the guy's lips, what Wyatt's face was like when he was cumming, and how he left the way he left. There wasn't anything he didn't tell. "I'm sorry I didn't say anything before. I knew you'd think I was crazy."

"Is that why you aren't seeing your family?"

"What do you mean?"

"I thought you guys were talking again."

"Nothing bad happened with them. I just haven't seen them for a while."

"Maybe it's because of him?"

"I don't think so."

"Were you seeing him because I wasn't around?"

"It has nothing to do with you. I should've told you. I never thought I'd be doing that stuff."

Lots of people were passing by on Church Street. Michael noticed them, but he wasn't looking at any faces.

"Do you like it?"

"Like what?"

"That leather stuff."

"People do those things."

"So you do like it? I'm not going to judge."

"I guess I like it," he said.

Nathan drank some of his beer. "To be honest, that guy—what's his name?"

"Wyatt."

"He sounds like a cult leader or something." Nathan laughed, but he sounded worried. "I don't know anything about that stuff. Bondage or whatever, but I don't think it's supposed to be like that. It sounds like there was something wrong with that guy. There are lots of people into leather who aren't crazy. I have a friend who likes it, but he's normal. Wyatt doesn't sound normal."

"Yeah. You're right."

"It sounds like you miss him."

"A bit."

"How old is he?"

"Older."

"How old?"

"I can't remember. Not twice my age but close."

"I'm not going to say what you should do, but if I were you, I'd stay away from him. Does he still message you?"

"It was just yesterday."

"Has he messaged you?"

"Yeah, but I haven't read them."

"I'd block him, but that's me."

"Okay."

Nathan looked down at their empty drinks. There was enough left in the pitcher to fill a third of each glass. "Do you want another pitcher?"

"Sure."

Nathan leaned over the table, waiting for a server to come by. "When you stop seeing someone, it's hard," he said. "Even if you ended it, you're going to miss them."

"I know."

Silence.

"Do we have to start going to leather bars now?"

Michael laughed. "Fuck you."

"Seriously. I think I'd look good in a harness. I almost bought one once."

"We don't need to go to a leather bar."

"I feel like we're too young to be getting into leather, but maybe not. I'd go with you if you want."

"Let's talk about something else," Michael said.

"I'm just fucking with you."

"I know."

"Are you okay?"

"I'm fine."

"Don't let anyone treat you like that."

"I didn't. I left."

o

Michael promised himself that he'd never let anyone treat him the way Wyatt did. Even when he started missing him more, and when Wyatt kept texting him, he didn't call or text back.

He thought the more time that passed, the easier it'd get, but it was the opposite. Once he got back to how his life was before, he started thinking about him more. The stuff they were doing together had made his life feel like it was worth something, to be a part of this other world. Most people wouldn't get it; they weren't normal things they were doing, but that's why Michael liked it most. It let him act in a way most people wouldn't get, but it made him feel more himself. His mom had told him that he wouldn't live a normal life, and he knew it himself, he could feel it since he was kid, but Wyatt showed him that it was okay not to be normal. He could be different and be proud of being different, living a life that was different—that's what he was missing by not being around Wyatt.

He couldn't remember how many weeks passed since he saw him last. It was over a month at least. Even as time went on, Wyatt would send him texts. He wasn't sending them as much as he was before, and Michael still couldn't read them. He'd delete them because he was afraid that Wyatt would say something to make him cave and go back to him. Wyatt had given him a lot, and a part of him was grateful, but he still saw him as a selfish narcissist with a nasty streak. It was easier to delete the texts and not worry about it, but it wasn't getting better.

8

Michael got tickets for a party in the west end. It was an all-leather party, but the only leather he had were wrist restraints Wyatt had bought him from a store on Yonge Street, so he thought about going to that same shop to pick up something else to wear after he was done work.

He'd passed the place a bunch of times, but he'd never been inside. It was sandwiched between a sushi restaurant and a place that sold sneakers. He got a rush going in, opening the door, knowing that people on the street were seeing him entering a kink shop. He wondered if he looked like the sort of person who'd go into a place like that.

The smell of leather in there was heavy; it was like being smacked across the face with it. A woman at the counter shouted,

"Hi, hun!" She was dressed in jeans but had a leather corset on and her black hair was tied in a bun.

His lips said, "Hi," back, but nothing came out of his mouth.

It was a big store, narrow but long with leather gear lining both walls, and racks and displays all down the middle. Michael started on the right side of the store and worked his way back slowly. The first section was all harnesses. He didn't know there could be so many different kinds. There were thick ones that looked old school and thinner ones in all different colours. Some weren't even made of leather. He didn't know what they were made of, but he felt a pair, and they were more like spongy plastic.

He thought a harness would be good for the party, but he didn't have it in him to pick one up. He was looking at them, pushing them around, but he'd never worn a harness, so even if he grabbed one to try, he didn't know how to put it on.

The woman in the corset came up from behind him. "Do you need any help, hun?"

"Just looking."

"If you need help, let me know."

Michael shook his head and looked down at the ground until she left him alone.

There were dozens of restraints and wristbands past the harnesses. There were even metal shackles there, like the ones they'd sell as part of a Halloween prison costume. He picked them up to see how heavy they were. They weighed a lot more than he thought because they weren't the pretend kind.

He put them back down and went to the very back of the store where the hoods and leather face masks were. He found the one that Wyatt had bought him. He picked it up—it was the exact same one. The only difference was that it didn't have his name written on the inside tag. It made him happy holding it; all the good things he felt with Wyatt came back. He put his hand inside it, trying to fill it out, and lifted it so he was face-to-face with it. He tried to imagine what he looked like when he was wearing it. He knew how weird it was. It sometimes made him laugh thinking how weird wearing it was. He never thought he'd be that weird, but it made him feel good when his face was erased, unlocking something inside of him. It was weird but he couldn't think of anything else that let him feel like that.

Michael laughed. *It's so fuckin' weird*, he thought, but he wanted it. He took it up to the woman at the front. It wasn't even something he could wear out to the party. He didn't have the nerve and it'd be too hot to wear all night anyway. He got it just because he felt like he wanted it. He didn't know if he'd use it. He put it on the counter and didn't say anything. The woman asked if he needed to try it on, but he said it was fine and inserted his credit card in the machine. She put it in a black bag and walked around the counter to give it to him.

"Enjoy," she said.

He took the black bag home, but he didn't try the mask on. He put it under his bed and pulled out the wrist restraints that Wyatt had given him that he'd hid under there too. They were chunky and had metal loops on them so they could be connected. He didn't know if the restraints were enough to get into the party. He thought maybe he should've bought something else at the shop, but the mask was four hundred dollars. He couldn't have afforded to buy more than what he bought.

He went to his closet and got the leather boots he sometimes wore for work. They weren't fetish boots, but he figured that with jeans on it'd be hard to tell that they were work boots.

The party was in a warehouse near Lansdowne station. There was a lineup of people when he got there that went all the way down the side of the building. Most guys there were in head-to-toe leather. There was so much of it, Michael could smell it even being outside. He thought it'd be an older crowd, but most were young, some even younger than himself.

When Michael got to the front, the guy at the door asked if he knew it was a leather party. Michael said he did, that's why he was there. The bouncer looked him up and down, and said he needed to be wearing leather—that they had a dress code—so Michael showed him the restraints that were hidden under his sleeves.

"You here with anyone?" the bouncer asked.

"No, it's just me."

The guy said he could come in if he took his shirt off right there at the door, so Michael did and pushed it into his back pocket. The bouncer made him promise to keep it off.

Michael had been to raves years ago, but nothing like this. The place was the size of a stadium, with thousands of people dancing under dark lights. Smoke hissed out of machines and condensation dripped from the ceiling. The music sounded like two metal pipes being smashed together. Thousands of bodies moved to the beat, dancing in gangs, in all leather. A lot of them had shaved heads or crewcuts. It was hard to tell one from the next. Even up close it was hard to see faces because of how dark it was.

Michael found a large bar on the far side of the dance floor. It wasn't busy; most people were drinking water, not booze—the party was supposed to go to ten in the morning, so he wasn't surprised.

He asked the bartender for a double shot of vodka and a beer. He'd had a couple of drinks before leaving his place, but the crowd at the party sobered him up and he needed something more, so he downed the vodka and washed it down with beer.

He took a few steps, so he was at the edge of the dance floor and started dancing. He stayed far away from everyone else for the first few minutes, but the bodies were moving in waves and he found himself getting drawn in until he was surrounded by people.

The music got harder; it was like electricity moving through his bones. He was getting drawn farther into the crowd, and it started feeling like the room went on forever because he couldn't see the end of it in any direction. He kept dancing like the music was going to take him someplace special as long as he didn't stop.

He felt better the more he moved and the more he sweated, with his eyes half open.

The dark lights lifted—it was one a.m., but it felt like the sun was coming up already. The lights went from blues and purples to reds and yellows. The music changed again to a softer beat. Michael opened his eyes wide; it was like waking up. There were two drumbeats, some synths, and a bit of bass, but nothing else.

He started seeing the faces around him under the bright lights. There were thousands of them, sweaty, some wearing sunglasses. He was stomping and throwing his shoulders back and forward. Nobody stopped moving even though the lights were up. They couldn't stop moving; Michael was feeling it too. It was like they were small parts of a big machine and if they stopped it'd break down.

Michael's jeans and underwear were soaked in sweat and he could taste salt on his lips. His eyes were shuffling through the crowd, and he moved his feet so his body circled around slowly. Some guys were looking back, but he didn't see anyone he was interested in taking home, and he'd decided he didn't want to go home alone. They were all dull faces to him—shaved and trimmed to look the same. He was looking for something different.

The music got heavier again—the drums kept doubling so it sounded like a marching band moving through the warehouse. A red strobe light was hitting each beat.

Michael kept spinning—he wiped the sweat off his forehead and onto his jeans.

Everyone was moving quicker to try to keep up with the drums.

The red strobe was getting so fast that it was like one constant red light.

People started cheering. Some were punching the air and stomping the ground.

When the drums couldn't go any faster, most people stopped dancing. The strobes stopped too, so it was pitch black. There was some whistling and people were still stomping their feet but everything else stopped for a second. Then it all started again: the drums picked up and so did the strobes, but they were going slow.

This guy was grinning at Michael. He had a thick beard and a peaked officer's cap pulled down low. He was a big guy, burly with hair all over his chest and shoulders that was pasted to his skin with sweat.

The red strobes kept going on and off, a second each. Whenever the lights came back on the guy was a bit closer, moving through the cluster of people between them. He never let his eyes off Michael; he never stopped grinning either.

He got really close and stood over him, watching him. He wasn't smiling anymore. Michael liked him better when he wasn't smiling.

The guy leaned down. "Are you going to talk to me?"

"I was about to."

"What were you going to say?" He was grinning again.

"'Hi,' I guess."

"Hello."

"Are you having fun?"

"More fun now."

"You're a sexy guy."

"You think so?"

"Yeah," Michael said.

"You caught my attention once I saw you."

They started kissing without saying anything else. The guy's mouth tasted like peppermint but his body smelled like sweat.

He pulled his head back and looked Michael in the eye. "Are you on anything?"

"I just had a few drinks."

"No drugs?"

"No."

"Good boy."

"Why, are you?"

"Fuck no," he said.

He grabbed Michael by the waist. They weren't dancing; the guy was just holding him, keeping him close, and using his other hand to drink his beer.

"What's your name?" he said without looking at Michael.

"Mike."

"I'm Marshall."

"It's very nice to meet you."

"You want another drink?"

"Um, I guess," he said. He'd almost finished his beer. "Yeah, sure."

Marshall grabbed his hand and walked him through the crowd. Michael wasn't expecting that, but he didn't mind it. He thought it was kind of nice holding hands. He couldn't remember the last time he held hands with someone in public. Marshall led him out of the main room to a side bar that was quieter and asked what he wanted to drink.

"What are you having?"

"I'm going to move on to a rum and Coke."

"I'll have the same."

"A double?"

Michael smiled. "Sure."

There were a bunch of guys around the bar waiting to get a drink too, but Marshall pushed his way through to the front. From far away, Michael thought he looked like a brute. He liked the idea of being with such a big boy with big biceps and a bit of a belly, who could overpower him.

When he came back with their drinks, he kissed Michael before he gave him his. "There you go, boy."

"What did you say?"

"Boy. That's what you are, isn't it?"

Michael shrugged; nobody had ever called him that but Wyatt. He thought Wyatt had made it up; he didn't know it was a thing.

"How can you tell?"

"You have that look."

Michael shrugged again and had some of his drink. It tasted like pure rum and made him cough. "It's strong."

"They know how to pour drinks here. They usually don't pour real drinks in Canada. This is like back home."

"You're not from here?"

"Ann Arbor. Do you know it?"

"I think I heard of it."

"It's close to Detroit. I drove here."

"Oh, okay."

"It's not a long drive."

"Are you here for a holiday?"

"Yeah. I come here a lot."

They were talking in the middle of where people were trying to pass, so Marshall took him to the side to a bunch of seats. They could still hear the music, but it felt like it was coming from somewhere far away.

"Do you like being called, 'boy'?" Marshall said, sitting down.

"I guess."

"Do you want me to call you 'boy'? You do, don't you? I can tell."

"Yeah."

"Do you like it?"

"I like it."

"I knew when I saw you, you wanted to be *my* boy. I could tell."

Michael smiled and let him kiss him again. He didn't smell like peppermint anymore, just sweat. The smell was everywhere. Michael put on too much deodorant to smell like that, but Marshall was the opposite—it was like he'd never worn deodorant before. Michael never liked the smell of body odour, but right now it was making him crazy. He was grabbing at Marshall, feeling his chest and belly. His hands were covered in Marshall's sweat like he was bleeding all over him.

Marshall lifted his head. "You're coming to Ann Arbor?"

"I guess so."

"If you're my boy you're coming."

Michael wanted to keep kissing him. "I'm coming, sir."

"How'd you know I like being called sir?"

"I don't know." He tried kissing him, but Marshall wouldn't let him.

"You know."

"You look like a sir."

"Good answer."

Marshall told him to kiss his neck so he did, then he said his chest, so Michael went down and liked the sweat from his pecs. Marshall lifted his arm, and the smell got really strong. Michael went for it and licked his armpit without Marshall having to ask him to.

"Good boy," Marshall moaned. "Attaboy."

It didn't really taste like anything, but it was where the most smell was.

"I'm going to send you home smelling like me, boy," Marshall chuckled.

"Yes, sir."

"That's if I ever let you go home. I might pack you up in my trunk and take you back with me. Would you like that, boy?"

"Yes, sir."

"Be careful what you wish for, boy. Now finish your drink." He grabbed it from the floor and handed it to him. "You'll like Ann Arbor. You been to Michigan, boy?"

"I've always wanted to."

"I might make you move there, boy. Finish your drink and let's go dance."

Michael sucked down the rest of his rum, then shook the plastic cup in the air. "It's finished."

"Good boy."

Marshall grabbed his hand and walked him toward the middle of the dance floor. They were being smeared in other people's sweat along the way. When they got to the middle, Marshall turned Michael around so his chest was against Michael's back. He wrapped his arms over his shoulders, and they started dancing like that. It was making Michael hard again, to be so close. Marshall must have known it would because he reached down into his pants and grabbed his dick.

"Fuck, boy," he said in his ear. "Is that all for Daddy?"

"Yes, sir."

"I got a lot of needs. I want a boy who can satisfy them all. Do you think you can do that, boy?"

Michael laughed; he was drunk. "I can, sir," he said. He didn't know what he meant, but he didn't want to kill the mood.

"Good boy."

They kissed some more, and then Marshall asked if he wanted to go back to his hotel room.

"Sure," Michael said.

When they left the place and went out to the street, they put their shirts back on.

There was a line of cabs waiting outside. Marshall grabbed Michael's hand and pulled him to one.

"Holiday Inn," he said to the cab driver, who had his window down.

"Which one?"

"I don't know which one. Downtown."

"There are two downtown."

He took out the room card from his pocket. "Carlton Street." He shook his head like the cab driver was being stupid, grabbed Michael's hand again and they both got inside.

"You have fun?" Marshall said.

"Yeah."

"More fun now that you met me?"

Michael smiled. The cab driver was making him shy.

"No?" Marshall said.

"Yeah."

"Good boy."

Michael thought he was going to hold his hand through the lobby. It was quiet, just after two a.m. There were some younger people eating pizza slices on the lobby sofas, looking like they just got back from partying too, but there was no one else down there. Still, Marshall didn't hold his hand.

When they got up to his room, Marshall warned him that it was a bit messy. There were things all over the place inside. His suitcase was opened in the corner with clothes hanging out of it. There were two twin beds, and one had the covers wrapped in itself and the other had leather gear piled on top: there were harnesses, boots and caps. On the TV stand, there were two empty cans of Budweiser.

"Do you want a beer?" Marshall said, going to the bed with the leather on it. He started tossing the gear over to the suitcase like he was trying to tidy up.

"Sure."

"They're in there." He pointed at the mini-fridge by the TV.

Michael grabbed a can. "Do you want one?"

"Sure," he said, sitting down at the side of the bed.

Michael opened the can for him and brought it over.

"You're the best boy, aren't you?"

"I guess so, sir."

"I know so. Aren't you going to remove Daddy's boots?" He stretched his feet out so his boots were balancing on his heels.

"Yes, sir." Michael chugged some of his beer first; being in the hotel room was making him sober, and he needed something to make him feel how he was feeling before. He took another mouthful before putting it down and getting on his hands and knees. He crawled halfway across the room to Marshall.

"Someone trained you well, boy."

When he got to his feet, he put the right one on his lap and started to untie the boot.

"That's a good boy." He moaned.

Michael pulled the boot off and put it next to him. He took Marshall's sock off too and stuffed it in the boot.

Marshall pushed his bare foot into Michael's crotch. "Getting hard yet, boy?"

"Getting there, sir."

Marshall's hat fell off his head. It was the first time Michael had seen him without it on—his head was shaved down to the skin. "I forgot I had that on," he laughed.

Michael grabbed his other boot, and started untying it too. It took him a bit of time because they'd been tied on tighter and there was a knot in the lace. Marshall was watching him this time. He was smiling, then he said, "What do you do for work, boy?"

Michael thought he'd heard wrong—he kept untying his boot. "What do you do for work?" he said again.

"What do you mean, sir?"

"Your job."

"Oh. I work in advertising."

"So you're a smart boy?"

Michael laughed. "I don't know if advertising means smart."

"You went to college?"

"Yeah."

"Then you're smart. I like smart boys."

"Thank you, sir."

"You're my smart boy."

Michael reached for his beer. He grabbed the can and took a sip.

"I never went to school, but I'm street smart. I'm a cabinet-maker," he said. "Got my own business in Ann Arbor."

Michael didn't really know what a cabinetmaker was. He thought maybe it had something to do with wood, but he didn't want to get into it so he put his beer down next to him and pulled the other boot off.

"I don't know if I should let you cum," Marshall said. "If I let you cum, you might not want to see me again." He laughed but he meant it, Michael knew it. His face changed; it was like his eyes were frowning and his lips were stiff. Michael couldn't look at him like that; he started rubbing his foot. He didn't like seeing him that way and Michael wanted to say something to make him feel better, but he didn't want to say anything he didn't mean.

"I like you," Michael said, rubbing his foot even harder.

"I know you do."

"I was looking for someone tonight, and turned out to be you." He was sure he meant it.

Marshall relaxed, leaning back on the headboard. He closed his eyes while Michael kept rubbing his foot and smiled like he was smiling before. He was still scared though. Michael could see it through his bushy beard. Everything about him was relaxed except his cheeks—they were shaking. Michael thought something must've happened to him to make him act like that. He didn't know what it was, but it made him wonder if it could ever happen to him. Marshall didn't look like someone who would be so scared. He was a brute with his big arms, shoulders, and a belly rolling over, and there was hair coming out from his shirt collar and sleeves, but he suddenly looked so small.

Michael rubbed his foot harder. "I want to make you happy, sir."

"I know you do, boy," Marshall said. "If you could have anything tonight, boy, what would it be?"

"To make you happy, sir."

Marshall opened his eyes and laughed. That made him happy like Michael knew it would—he was a little less scared.

"I want to be inside my boy," Marshall said, getting serious.

"If that's what you want, I want it too."

"Good. Then stand up and take your clothes off, boy."

Michael did as he was told, but while he was doing it, Marshall got up and undressed too.

"What do you think of your sir?" Marshall said flexing both biceps at once.

"I think I'm lucky, sir."

"I'm lucky too, boy. We're both lucky." He pushed Michael onto the bed, got on top, and started kissing him. Michael reached for his shaved head and ran his hands over it. He liked the feeling of shaved skin on his fingers.

They were kissing like they were in love, moving their tongues with intent. Michael kept his hands on Marshall's head the whole time. His forehead was sweating. It felt like the air conditioner was on high, but Michael kept mopping the sweat with his palms.

Marshall lifted his legs and started fucking him like that. The smell from his body came back, but it was stronger than it was before. Michael closed his eyes and felt his body buzz from the smell and the feeling of Marshall moving in and out of him.

Marshall turned Michael around so his face was in the mattress and used Michael's wrist restraints to bind his hands behind his back. "I'm going to give it to you, boy," he said. He fucked Michael like that from behind, going at him even harder.

"I need you, sir," Michael said.

"I need you too, boy."

Michael's breathing got heavy; he couldn't control it. He started thrusting his hips at the same time Marshall was pushing in so that he could get deeper. Michael could taste Marshall's odour; it was making him dizzy. He started cumming without touching himself. That'd never happened before—it was like something else had taken him over.

When Marshall noticed, he started fucking him quicker. "I'm going to breed you, boy," he said. "Boy oh boy, you're getting it all." It only took a few seconds for him to cum too so that they were both groaning at the same time.

"Fuck, boy! Fuck!" Marshall said.

He undid Michael's restraints and fell next to him. He was still catching his breath. Michael's body dropped too and he started laughing as he stretched his arms out.

"What?" Marshall said, lifting his head.

"That was so good. Thank you, sir."

It was still dark out, but Michael could hear birds singing from outside the window. "What time is it?" he said.

Marshall cleared his throat. "I don't know."

"I guess it doesn't matter."

"No. Are you going to sleep with me, boy?"

"If that's what you want."

"Thank you."

o

Michael woke up with Marshall's arms wrapped around him. He couldn't stay asleep like that so he wiggled his way out and moved to the other bed. He closed his eyes again and drifted in and out of sleep for the next hour, for as long as he could, but then he was wide awake.

The curtains were closed, but he could tell it was sunny out because of the glow coming from them. He got out of bed without waking Marshall and grabbed his phone from his jeans on the floor to check the time. It was after eleven o'clock—he hadn't meant to sleep in that late and had things he needed to get done.

He went back to the bed and leaned over. "Are you up?" he whispered. He could tell by his breathing that Marshall was deep asleep.

"Marshall, you up?" It looked like he'd be asleep for a while too, but he figured if he was on vacation he should sleep in if that's what he wanted to do.

Michael grabbed his clothes from the floor and was quiet about putting them on so he wouldn't wake Marshall. He left a note for him saying that he tried waking him but couldn't and had to run. He included his phone number and email and said that if he was free later on, they should get together. He thanked him, said he had fun, and told him that he wanted to see him again. He signed the letter, "Your boy."

He left the hotel, but once he was out the door, he realized he didn't bring his wrist restraints with him. He thought about going back, but he couldn't remember the room he came from and didn't want to wake Marshall anyway. He figured he'd hear from him. He had to be staying the whole weekend if he was on vacation. Even if he didn't get them back, it was for the best. He shouldn't have kept anything from Wyatt, so if he lost them, it was fine, but he was sure he'd get them back.

He could smell Marshall on him the whole way home. It didn't bug him. He liked the smell, and he didn't want to shower right away so he could keep smelling him.

He made coffee and toast when he got home and had it at his computer. He watched the news on YouTube but kept smelling his hands. He was starting to miss him because of it. Even though he was tired and hungover, he hadn't felt good like that since Wyatt. He wished he hadn't left Marshall's room; he was starting to think that he shouldn't have left because he was missing him so much and hoped Marshall didn't think it was bad that he didn't wait.

He couldn't shake Marshall from his head the whole day: when he went to the gym he was thinking about him, and when he got his hair cut and picked up groceries for the week, he thought of him too.

After he finished everything he needed to get done, he started worrying because Marshall still hadn't texted or emailed him. It was close to five and he figured he would've heard back from him by now. There was no way he was still sleeping.

Michael made dinner and watched a movie while he ate, but he kept checking his phone every five minutes hoping for a text. He figured Marshall didn't like how he left, and that he should've waited. Everything else went well. Why didn't he text?

By nine that night it was really bugging him and he figured he had to do something about it. He washed up, put on a nice shirt and some jeans, and he walked back over to the hotel. He didn't know the room number but remembered that he was on the fifth floor, so he snuck by the front desk and went to the elevators. He thought if he went up, he'd remember the way to the room just by being up there. He was going to apologize, and say that he shouldn't have left the way he did; he was going to promise not to leave like that again—that's what he was going to say. It'd been a long time since he felt that good—he'd say that too.

He got out of the elevator and hoped he'd see something that'd help him remember the room, but there were four different ways to go, and they all looked the same. He couldn't tell which direction he'd come from that morning so he walked down one of the halls. He could've come out of any of the doors. He tried the other halls too, but it was all the same and he knew that unless he knocked on every door—which he half-considered—he wasn't going to find him.

He went back down to the lobby and thought to ask for him at the front desk. He knew his first name and where he was from but didn't want to tell the person at the desk what had happened—he didn't have it in him. He needed to make something up, so he went to the front desk and said that he was talking to a Marshall from Ann Arbor, Michigan, at the pub down the street. Marshall forgot his phone when he left, he knew he was staying at the hotel, and he wanted to get it back to him.

"Oh no!" the worker said. "Marshall from Ann Arbor?" He started tapping on the computer. "Marshall Charles?"

"Marshall Charles—it could be. He's from Ann Arbor?"

"Yep, do you want me to call up?"

"I can just go up."

"I'm sorry, sir, we can't let people up without calling first."

"Makes sense."

The worker called, balancing the phone between his shoulder and ear. "Sorry, he's not answering."

"Oh, maybe he's out."

"Or he's sleeping."

"Right. Okay. Maybe I'll come back."

"You should probably leave the phone here."

"I want to give it to him myself."

"He would need his phone."

"I'll come back, I'm not far from here."

"Sir, please leave the phone. Not having a phone in a new city isn't good. Why didn't you leave it at the bar?"

"What do you mean?"

"He probably went back to the bar looking for it."

"I didn't think of that."

"It's probably the first thing he did." He grabbed an envelope from under the desk. "I'll put it in this and leave it for him."

Michael grabbed his own phone and handed it over. He left a note with it, saying he was sorry for leaving without waking him up; it was dumb of him to do and said that he'd explain the phone thing. He said to send an email since he didn't have his phone anymore. He knew his last name anyway, so he could try coming back again in the worst case.

Michael left the hotel and walked down to Church Street. He wondered if he was out having a drink, so he stopped by Woody's on the way. It was one of those spots that everyone would start their nights at before heading off somewhere else.

It was still early, but there were lots of people there already. He took his time walking around, keeping an eye out for Marshall. He circled the place twice to make sure he didn't miss him, but he wasn't there, he was sure of it. It didn't mean he wasn't coming. It was still early, so he went to the front bar and ordered a beer. He could keep an eye out for people coming and going from the front. It wasn't the only way to get into the place. There was a smaller entrance at the other bar, but he figured he'd do another wander around when he finished his drink in case he came in from there.

There were five to ten guys coming in at a time, but Michael made sure to look at all of their faces so he wouldn't miss him. Some guys would notice him looking and smile; he'd smile back, but it wasn't what he was there for so he'd keep the smile brief and continue scanning the faces of the guys coming in.

He finished his drink, so he ordered another and walked through the place again. It was getting harder to move because there were so many guys coming through. Even in the last twenty minutes, the number of people had doubled. He had to move slowly because he didn't want to miss him if he was there. He tried not to bump into anyone or spill his drink, but it wasn't easy. He stopped at the back bar facing the stage. A drag queen was up there, getting ready for a show. It was too much work to try to get to the front again, so he finish his drink back there.

They put the music down low and shined a light on the drag queen onstage. She was wearing a silver sequinned gown and had a red curly wig on.

She tapped on the microphone a few times to make sure it worked.

"Good evening, Woody's!" she said. "Can you motherfuckers hear me?" She kept tapping on the microphone.

"YES!" the crowd shouted back.

She put her hands above her eyes to block the spotlight. "Such a beautiful crowd tonight. So beautiful. Obviously, I'm drunk: you're probably all ugly fucks, but you look beautiful to me right now—everybody is beautiful!—so let's keep it that way! Jess, can you get me a fuckin' vodka?" She was talking to the bartender, who started pouring her a drink. "A double. I need to keep these ugly bitches looking good." Everyone was looking at the bartender now. She didn't say anything until he brought it to her.

"Thank you, dear," she said. "Meet me in the back alley in ten minutes for some *sucky sucky*. I'll take care of *you*, baby." People laughed some more. She acted surprised that they could hear her. "What?! Oh fuck you, you're all fuckin' ugly whores."

Michael got this feeling that Marshall wasn't there, and that he wasn't going to come no matter how long he waited. Yeah, he shouldn't have left in the morning the way he did, but it's not like he disappeared. He left a note with his number. He tried him at the hotel—he didn't have his phone anymore because he wanted to see him. He couldn't feel bad about it. He did everything he could and after all that if he still didn't hear from him, he figured it was the way it had to be.

He pushed his way back to the front bar and finished his drink standing at the side. He could still see the drag queen from where he was. She was lip-syncing to a song now. It was one he knew, but he couldn't name it. He thought maybe it was Céline Dion.

"You're taking way too long to talk to me," he heard someone say. He thought it was Marshall, even though it wasn't his voice.

He turned; it definitely wasn't him.

"Sorry, are you talking to me?" Michael said.

"I said . . . it felt like . . . ." The guy's face turned red. "I mean, I thought you were never going to talk to me."

"Me?"

"Aye."

Michael chuckled. "Okay. Sorry about that."

"Ah, don't beat yourself up over it." The guy grabbed Michael's hand and grasped it tightly. He gave it a shake. "I'm Calum."

"What is it?"

"Calum."

"That's your name?"

"It is."

"What sort of name is that?"

"Are you taking the piss?"

"What? No. I mean where is it from?"

"It's Scottish. Can't you tell by my accent?"

"I can't hear an accent?"

"Don't tell me I've lost my accent."

"I can't hear anything. The music is too loud." Michael pointed to the drag queen.

"Should I speak louder so you can hear it?" he said. He was being serious.

"I think I can hear it now that I'm listening for it."

Calum looked like he was going to say something else but he stopped and tapped his foot to the music. He was very clean looking with his blue shirt tucked into his jeans. It was a collared shirt with only the top button undone and the sleeves rolled up. The colour of it matched his eyes; it had to be on purpose.

"Anyway, have a good night," Michael said, throwing back the rest of his drink.

"Ah, you need another."

"I don't think that's what I need."

"Come on now, let me buy you another, please." He started playing with his ear, folding it into itself. "Just a wee pint."

Michael could've used another drink anyway. He had nothing else to do other than go home and check his email. "I could have one more."

Calum ordered them some beer and lifted his glass. "Cheers." He waited for Michael to do the same. "And you need to make eye contact or you'll suffer seven years of bad sex. You don't want that."

"No, I don't." Michael looked him in the eye; it made Calum blush. "Cheers again." They smacked their glasses together. "Thanks for the drink. You didn't have to."

"Don't worry about it."

"How long have you been here?"

Calum looked at his watch. "No more than an hour. Same time as you, I think."

"No, in the city? You said you're from Scotland. Are you on vacation?"

"I was supposed to be here for six months, but it's been six years now. You lot can't get rid of me, can ya?"

"Why did you come to Toronto?"

"I was doing a semester here at the university, you see."

"Why did you stay?"

"For a job. I'm a lawyer. I'm one of the good guys though." He elbowed Michael. "I practice environmental law. I work the system from the inside."

"You're working the system from the inside?"

"Aye, I go to protests. You know, but you have to be in the system to make real changes." He was about to say something else but he stopped talking. Then he said, "I've had a wee bit to drink. If my chat is rubbish you can say so."

"What you said actually makes sense."

"I guess I'm not just a pretty face, am I?"

"Guess not."

"I think you're handsome. I saw you walking around in circles all night. I figured you were looking for me, you just didn't know it."

Michael laughed.

"I swear on my mother's life."

"Right. Yeah, I've been looking for days."

"I knew it! Weeks probably. Years! You're lucky to have found me after all this time. You've probably been lost without me."

"So lost."

Calum smiled. "I can tell."

The drag queen on stage grabbed a rain jacket and umbrella from the side and started singing "It's Raining Men" by the Weather Girls next. She wasn't lip-syncing; she was singing it live. Calum started mouthing the words, and when the song got going, he closed his eyes and used his fist as a microphone. He was lip-syncing so hard it was like the words were coming out of his mouth. Michael was embarrassed for him but at the same time, he liked that he could let go like that.

The drag queen had two shirtless men dancing behind her who had umbrellas too. She was making funny faces at them while she was singing, and the people watching from the front were shouting the words back at her.

Michael finished his drink before Calum could get through half of his. He was drinking fast, and when Calum noticed, he said, "Another drink?"

"I should go," he said.

"Go where?"

"Home."

"We just met though."

"I was out last night late."

"Can I at least get your phone number?"

"I lost my phone tonight."

"You lost your phone? Is that a hint?"

"Serious. It's a long story. I do need to go home."

"Can I get your email then? Anything—don't make me beg."

"Give me your phone," he said. He wrote his email in it and gave him his phone number too. He told him again that he lost his phone so if he tried texting and didn't hear back, that's why.

Before Michael left, Calum gave him a kiss on the cheek but asked if it was okay after he did it.

"It's fine," Michael said.

○

Michael got home and poured himself half a glass of wine. He wanted to check his email but was nervous that Marshall didn't send anything. He stayed in the kitchen with his drink, leaning against the counter, trying to *feel* out whether Marshall had messaged him, like he was psychic and would know without checking. It's not that he felt Marshall didn't message him, but he didn't feel that he did either—he was trying to read what his gut was telling him.

He finished his wine, poured a little more, and took his glass to his computer, which was sitting on the sofa. He opened his email; there was one new message. It was from Marshall:

*I DIDN'T LIKE HOW YOU LEFT BOY. YOU SHOULD
KNOW BETTER BUT I LIKE THAT YOU CAME
TO THE HOTEL. I WILL BE AT THE EAGLE BAR.
COME AND MAKE IT UP TO ME BOY.*

He didn't even think to check the Eagle. It was the only leather
bar in town—if he was going to be anywhere, it'd be there, but it
hadn't crossed his mind.

Michael caught a cab back to Church Street. Marshall had
emailed him two hours ago—he figured he'd still be there. It was
only eleven o'clock.

He got to the Eagle in less than ten minutes, but there was a
big line outside. He went to the back and asked the group in front
of him how long they'd been waiting. They couldn't remember
but said that they were only letting people inside if someone came
out. It took close to forty minutes to get in.

The place was packed, shoulder to shoulder. The only light
was coming from the bar at the side, and the TVs that were set
up behind it that were playing porn. He'd never been to this bar,
and it wasn't as big as he thought it'd be. It was long and narrow and the back half of it had a small dance floor that was just
as full as the front. He didn't find Marshall back there. He went
through the dance floor twice. It wasn't big; if he was back there
he would've seen him, so he went to the front bar again, but he
wasn't there either. It was busy, but it'd be impossible to miss him
if he was there.

He noticed a set of stairs by the washroom. He asked the
bouncer who was guarding it if there was anything up there; it's
where the patio was. He went up through the dark stairs to the
rooftop patio, which was fenced in with boards of wood painted
black and string lights crossing overhead. It was just as busy
upstairs as it was down, and just as narrow. There were benches
all along the walls, but it was impossible to see who was sitting
because of everyone standing around.

He checked the benches on the left side, but he didn't see Marshall. He checked the right side, from the front of the patio to the back—he wasn't there either. He figured he'd left already; it was getting late. He checked the back benches anyway, and could only see his head; there was a big group between them. He waved to get his attention, but Marshall didn't notice. Michael got closer but saw that he wasn't alone. There was a young guy leaning into his chest who was wearing a leather harness and black baseball cap. Marshall had his arm resting across his stomach, and he was twisting the guy's nipple with his other hand.

Michael didn't get any closer. He regretted the way he left that morning; he wouldn't do something like that again, but everyone makes mistakes.

There was nothing else he could say, so he took a few steps back. Marshall still didn't see him, and was he whispering in the guy's ear now. It made Michael feel replaceable. Maybe he was? Everyone was. That's what he started thinking, but it didn't make him feel any better.

Maybe he shouldn't have left how he left, but there was a note there for him. Marshall was on vacation. He didn't want to wake him. Michael's number was on the note. It wasn't that bad. It could've been worse. He went back to his hotel and tried to find him. He left his phone there—that's how much he wanted to find him, and Marshall just replaced him. Michael would've gone to Ann Arbor—he was serious about that. He hated being replaced. It made him feel like he was nothing. Wyatt had probably replaced him too—he was probably with another boy right now.

He went back down the stairs and out the door. His fists were clenched, and he caught himself stomping his feet down the street—he probably looked stupid, he knew it, but he didn't care. There was a lot that was stupid. He thought how the leather thing was stupid—it was dumb, grown men talking in scripts, saying "sir" and "boy" like it meant something. They weren't even acting themselves—they were trying to be something more than what they were. "Bullshit, it's all bullshit," he said out loud, over and over again. He was still stomping his feet.

When he got to the Church and Wellesley intersection, the light turned red so he stopped walking. He still needed his phone. He didn't want to go back, but if he just got his phone from Marshall, he'd have it and he wouldn't need to try to get it tomorrow.

The light turned green, but he didn't move. It made sense to go back. He turned around but heard the sound of knocking on glass. It was Calum sitting in the burger shop at the corner, knocking at the window from the other side. He waved and smiled, so Michael waved back. He could hear him shouting to come in. Michael stood there and stared, so Calum got up and went to the door. He held it open with his hip.

"I thought you were going home," he said.

"I did—I got an email about my phone so I came out again."

"Did you find it?"

"No."

"Oh. Well, are you hungry?" Calum had this goofy smile. Michael could tell he was drunk by his smile. "Can I buy you a burger?"

"I could eat."

°

Michael woke up not knowing where he was. He lifted up his head. Everything around him was black or white: the duvet and bed sheets, pillows, walls—they were one colour or the other, like a checkerboard. Then he remembered going home with Calum, taking a cab to his place. They ate their food, got in a cab, had some more drinks at his place, but they must've been strong drinks because that's the most Michael could remember.

Calum wasn't there, so he got up and opened the bedroom door. He could hear him cooking something down the hall in the kitchen. It smelled like eggs and toast too. He quietly walked down the hall and found Calum at the stove with his back to him.

"Good morning," Michael said.

Calum turned with the pan in his hand. "I was going to surprise you." He kept moving the sausages around in the pan with a spatula.

"I'm surprised."

"I was going to bring it to you in bed."

"You didn't have to make breakfast."

"Why?"

"I just meant you didn't have to."

"I wanted to," he said, emptying the sausages onto two plates he had set out on the counter, which already had eggs and toast on them.

"It looks good."

"You were cute yesterday. I was trying to romance you on the sofa and you fell asleep on me."

"Is that what happened?"

"Aye, you don't remember?"

"No."

"I carried you to bed. You don't remember?"

"It's a big blank."

"Funny that. I put you in the guest room. I didn't think it was right to put you in my bed."

"I would've been okay with it."

"We hadn't even kissed yet. I didn't know what to do."

"We still haven't kissed?"

"You don't remember if we kissed or didn't kiss?"

"I don't think we did."

"But you don't remember?"

Michael laughed. "No."

"Well, you don't remember because we didn't, but I was going to try on the sofa before you fell asleep."

"You can kiss me now, but I don't think my breath is too great."

"Your breath makes no difference to me. I've been wanting to kiss you for twelve hours now."

"Then kiss me. It's the least I can do since you put me up for the night."

"Ah, is that all it is?" He got that goofy smile again from last night. Michael thought it was how he looked when he was drunk, but it was just how he smiled.

Calum asked what he took in his coffee.

"Just black," Michael said.

Calum handed him the mug and kissed him. Michael was careful not to spill his drink, holding it out to the side. He stopped kissing for a second to put it down, then started again and untied the string of Calum's shorts. He pulled at the elastic to get his hand down there, but Calum stopped him.

"Easy, easy," he said. "We're only just kissing." His face turned red. It made Michael embarrassed too.

"Sorry."

"Don't be sorry. I like it. I just don't want breakfast to get cold. Are you hungry?"

"I'm always hungry."

Michael let go and took his coffee to the table, which Calum had set with napkins and cutlery. It was a glass table with a purple orchid on it by the glass wall that looked back at the city. Calum's condo was high up. From the table, there was a view of downtown—a clear view but it was far. His place looked like it was on Yonge Street or close to it, but somewhere north.

"Is this our first date?" Michael said.

"We had our first date at the burger shop last night. Don't you remember?"

"I remember."

"What's the date?" Calum asked.

"What do you mean?"

"Yesterday's date—do you know it? We need to remember it so we can celebrate our anniversary next year."

"Next year? That's a long time away."

"Aye, but it'll be here sooner than you think."

"Should I be worried that you're already talking about our anniversary not even twelve hours in?"

"You just tried ravaging me, which is more worrying, I'm not going to lie. But I don't blame you. I've been told that I'm irresistible."

Michael laughed.

"What's so funny? If you can't help yourself I don't blame you. What are you laughing about?"

"So what's the date then?"

"August 21, of course."

"I can't believe it's already the end of August."

"You'll see, a year from now I'll be taking you out for a nice burger to celebrate."

o

Michael got back home at noon and showered. He made a sandwich for lunch and watched TV for a bit but then remembered to check his email because he still didn't have his phone. Marshall had sent another message, writing that he waited at the Eagle and was disappointed that Michael didn't come for him. He left Michael's cell phone with the hotel reception—even though he was disappointed, he thought he should have it back. He left for Michigan early that morning.

Michael wrote back, thanking him for the phone. He told him that he did go to the Eagle. He saw him with someone else and didn't want to bug him, so he didn't say anything—it looked like he was having fun—but he was sorry for how he left yesterday morning and said he'd learned his lesson. He didn't mean anything by leaving like that; he didn't want to wake him because he was on vacation. He wrote all that, trying to play up the guilt, and he knew it'd work. It made him feel good writing the note the way he did, and he felt sorry for Marshall, a grown man acting how he'd acted, but Michael knew he was being petty too in writing the note the way he did. He couldn't help himself.

o

It was a few days before he saw Calum next. He'd asked Michael if he wanted to go for dinner at the harbourfront after work, so they met on Lakeshore Boulevard. Calum hugged him and kissed him on the lips when he saw him. He didn't care that there were people around, and Michael didn't care either.

They walked along the lakeshore and talked about their weeks. Then they talked about the type of music they liked and concerts they've been to. Michael also asked where Calum would go if he wanted a night out. He listed a lot of the same places that Michael went to on Church Street, and they thought it was funny they'd never seen each other before.

Calum asked if he wanted to stop at a grassy spot by the water for a minute. They lay down and Calum kissed him again; they were both blinded by the setting sun. There were lots of people around them: families and groups of friends, kicking soccer balls and throwing frisbees and baseballs, but Michael and Calum were acting like nobody was there but them.

Calum was in a dress shirt that was tucked into his jeans. It started coming loose on one side when they were kissing with skin showing but he didn't fix it.

Michael started hearing the seagulls, and motorboats moving through the water. He could smell the grass and the lake.

Calum lifted his head and looked Michael in the eye. "You're lucky you found me, you know." He laughed.

Michael laughed too. "You're lucky you found me."

"Aye, quite lucky."

A soccer ball hit Calum's back. Michael looked up, thinking it was done on purpose—that whoever did it had something to say about them kissing.

Calum got up and grabbed the ball.

"Sorry," this kid said, running up to them. He was young with freckles and missing his two front teeth so he had a lisp.

His mom was right behind them. "So, sorry."

"Hey, listen, don't worry about it." Calum dropped the ball and passed it over to the kid.

"Say thank you," the mother said.

"Thank you."

Calum grinned like he got a kick out of it and turned to Michael. "Are you hungry?"

"I could eat."

They kept walking down to a patio Calum liked. He made Michael order fish and chips because he said it was as good as the fish and chips in Scotland. Michael didn't know that they did fish and chips there—he thought it was an English thing, but Calum said it was big there too. They didn't just eat haggis. "Everyone thinks we wear kilts all the time and eat haggis for every meal."

"Do you eat a lot of haggis?"

"Not a lot but sometimes. I can make it for you if you want to try."

They went back to Calum's after for some wine, and he put on Erasure; they were his favourite band—he said "Chains of Love" was their best song. When it came on, Calum started lip-syncing to it with his eyes closed, using his fist as a microphone like he did when they first met. Michael knew that if he wanted to love Calum, he would let him, and watching him pretend to sing, he felt he could love him. Everything about him was lovable.

When he opened his eyes again, he stopped mouthing the words and kissed Michael. He was so innocent—that's what Michael started thinking. More innocent than him. Calum had been through things that all queer people go through—during dinner they'd compared coming out stories and it wasn't easy for him either. He wasn't disowned, but it took time for his parents to come around, and Calum didn't say this, but Michael wondered if he'd left the U.K. because of it. He didn't know him well enough to ask, but even with all that, he stayed innocent and being around him made Michael see that innocence was something he'd lost himself. He wanted to protect Calum and love him so he'd never lose it the way he did. Calum was older, but he was younger inside.

When they got naked, Calum said he wanted to fuck him. They'd never fucked before. The first time they just kissed and sucked each other off, but when Calum said he wanted to fuck him, Michael said, "Then fuck me."

Calum was gentle with him, like Michael was made of glass. Michael was on his hands and knees on the sofa with Calum behind. He started kissing his neck while he fucked him, being romantic about it. Michael didn't mind it. They fucked and after they came, Michael put his arms around Calum, holding him like a baby.

They saw each other almost every other day after that. They'd go to Michael's place or Calum's and take turns making dinner for each other. They'd always do a sleepover and fuck before bed. They started making a routine of it. The first time, they fucked on the couch, but that was the only time. After that they'd do it in bed before they went to sleep, and Calum was always very careful with him. Michael would've liked it better if Calum treated him rough and joked one time that he liked to be choked. Calum couldn't tell if he meant it or not, and when he asked, Michael just laughed.

9

Calum kept saying he wanted to take Michael to Toronto Island. He hadn't been there in years and knew. Michael liked to go. They planned to meet where the ferries went out, Michael arrived there first. There was a big line of people, so he joined it instead of waiting for Calum because it looked like it'd be a long wait.

His phone buzzed in his pocket, and he figured it was Calum, so Michael picked up and said, "Where are you, sexy?"

"Habibi?"

"Oh, who is this? Mom?"

"Hi, habibi. It's me."

She'd been calling, leaving lots of messages. He wasn't picking up because he decided he didn't like talking on the phone. He wouldn't call back either. Nothing bad had happened between them; he just decided he didn't like the phone. He believed it had nothing to do with her. He never talked on the phone; he was mostly texting with Calum or Nathan—he just didn't like talking to anyone.

"Hi, Mom."

"I was ready to leave another message."

"Sorry, I've been busy."

"It's okay." Silence. "I missed you. It's good to hear your voice."

"I missed you too," Michael said.

"When do I get to see you?" she said.

"I'm just about to go to Toronto Island with friends. I have stuff going on tomorrow too."

"I can make you dinner next weekend."

He didn't feel like going. He was trying to think if he had anything next weekend to give him a reason not to go.

"You don't want to see your mama?" She started laughing, but it didn't sound like a joke.

"It's not that."

"I miss my baby."

He couldn't remember the last time he was over. It'd been a long time, but he didn't want to go. He didn't like how he felt when he was there, but he felt pressure to visit, a pressure that came from himself. He figured he should because it was the right thing to do. He couldn't be the one not trying to make it work.

He said he'd come next weekend, but figured if he didn't feel like it by then, he would cancel. It wasn't a big deal to say he'd go. It made her happy to hear—it cost him nothing. She asked what he felt like eating, naming off Lebanese dishes in Arabic. "I'll make whatever my baby wants."

Michael noticed Calum crossing through the parkette next to the ferry line. He waved to get his attention and Calum waved back. "I don't know, Mom," he said. "Why don't you pick? I'll eat anything."

"There's nothing that you want, my baby?"

"I can't think of anything."

Calum was about to kiss him, but he pointed to the phone.

"What about warak enab?"

He hadn't had it in a while so he said, "Yeah, sure."

"Are you coming alone?"

"What do you mean?"

"We can talk about these things now."

"What things?"

"If you have a partner."

"What do you mean?"

"You call it a partner? Or a boyfriend?"

Michael didn't say anything; he didn't want to be talking about this right now.

"Do you have a boyfriend?"

"There's someone."

He didn't know what he and Calum were. They'd been seeing each other for a little bit now, so he wasn't lying when he said what he said, but they'd never talked about it. Michael didn't think they needed to. He was having fun and Calum was as well; he didn't think it mattered more than that.

"You can tell me stuff like this, habibi," his mom said. "Is he going to come with you?"

She was acting like it was normal to talk about this stuff. He didn't know where it was coming from. It wasn't what he wanted to be talking about, so he didn't say anything.

"If you want to bring him, he can come." Silence. "Would he be my son-in-law?" She laughed.

"Absolutely not."

"Anyone who you love, I love. I want my baby to be happy."

He needed to get off the phone; he had nothing else to say other than "We'll see, but I need to go, Mom."

She made him promise to come next weekend before he hung up. He said, "Yes, I promise."

"That was your mum?" Calum said.

"Yeah."

"How is she?"

"She's doing well. How are you?"

He grabbed his hip and kissed him. "Better now."

Calum was in shorts and a polo and wore a Toronto Blue Jays cap that was too big for his head. He had a backpack full of beers and sandwiches, and said he knew a quiet spot on the side of the island where nobody else went.

When they got on the ferry, there was nowhere to sit, but they found a place to stand near the front by a pole. Michael grabbed onto it when the boat got going, and Calum put his hand over his and squeezed. He listed off the sandwiches he got: roast beef, tuna, and ham, but asked if he ate ham.

"I eat everything," Michael said.

"I didn't know for sure." He squeezed his hand again. "Some Muslims don't, isn't that right?"

"I wouldn't say I'm Muslim. Maybe an agnostic Muslim?"

"A what?"

"Agnostic Muslim."

"You're a nutter, aren't ya? That's what I liked about you."

"I'll take that as a compliment."

"It is, trust me."

A breeze came through the cabin from the lake as the boat gained some speed. Michael closed his eyes. "That feels nice."

"It does."

The ferry turned toward the island and went even faster. Calum grabbed onto his hat so it wouldn't fly off.

"Your family is religious, are they?" Calum asked.

"Growing up I had to pray five times a day, fast during Ramadan, do all that."

"They're still like that?"

"Yeah, and my mom wears a hijab."

"I didn't know that."

"I never told you," Michael said, giving Calum a light shove with his shoulder. "So she asked if I'm seeing anybody. She's never asked that before."

"Did you tell her that you have a new Scottish lover?"

Michael shoved him again.

"You were talking about me, weren't ya?" Calum said.

Michael looked out at the island, which was getting closer. "I said I was seeing somebody."

"Your Scottish lover."

"Are we just lovers?"

"You want me to be your boyfriend, don't ya?"

"I didn't say that—I was just asking."

"You do want to be my boyfriend."

"You're such a weirdo."

"I'm not a weird-doe," he said as two separate words, like he'd never said it before.

"You're a weirdo."

"You're my boyfriend."

Michael smiled, then said, "She invited you for dinner next weekend if you have nothing else planned."

Calum got serious. "What day?"

"I'm guessing Saturday."

"I have nothing. I can go."

"You don't have to."

"I want to."

"Okay," Michael said. He looked at the island again, which was very close now. The ferry started pulling into the dock.

Calum said it was a bit of a walk to get to the spot he wanted to take him to. He said it was a good thing—that's why there was nobody there. It'd feel like they had the island to themselves.

They got off the ferry at Centre Island and crossed a big field that took them to the far side of it, past all the crowds. It was already starting to get quiet.

"It doesn't even feel like we're in the city anymore," Michael said.

"That's just it."

"I've been lots of times, but never to this part. Just to the gay part. The naked beach."

"You're a nudist?" Calum said.

Michael laughed. "No. I've tried going naked, but it wasn't for me. Even if you don't go naked, it's fun though. You can do anything there. Just have drinks or whatever."

"Aye, I went there once. It was busier than I expected."

"Were you naked?"

"I couldn't."

"I like it when you're naked."

"I don't feel like I want to be naked on a beach. If I wanted to I would, but I don't want to."

"That's fair," Michael said. "What about with sex?"

"What about it?"

"Is there sex stuff you never tried that you felt you wanted to try?"

"Like what?"

"Like anything."

"I don't know. What about you?"

"I've tried a lot of stuff."

"Really? Like what?"

"Just lots of stuff. But I asked you the question."

"I'm not going to lie, you've piqued my curiosity now."

"If you tell me, I'll tell you."

"I don't know." He had to think. "I've never been handcuffed."

Michael stopped walking. "Seriously?"

"What?

Michael shook his head and kept walking again. "Is that something you want to do?"

"Maybe. I've thought about it."

Michael laughed. "It hurts a lot more than you probably think."

"You've been handcuffed?"

"I said that I've tried lots of stuff."

They turned onto a sandy path that led up a small hill. Calum said that they weren't far. They crossed through a bunch of bushes to the other side where the beach was. There was no one else there, just some sailboats they could see out in the water, but that was it, the boats and them.

"Do you like it?" Calum said.

"Yeah, it's perfect."

"Aye, it's a special place."

"Thank you for bringing me," Michael said. He put his arms around Calum and kissed his cheek. "Do you bring all your lovers here?"

"You're not my lover, you're my boyfriend. And no. You're the first."

"I don't believe it."

"Believe it. You must feel special now, don't ya?"

Michael smiled.

"Let's have a beer to celebrate," Calum said. "I have a boyfriend now." He grabbed two cans from his backpack and gave Michael one. They sat on a big rock that was sticking out of the sand and had their beers. They were looking out to the water. The tree behind them shaded most of their bodies, except their legs, which were sticking out in the sun.

Michael closed his eyes and listened to the small waves rolling off the sand and seagulls circling over them.

"What do you want to try that you haven't done?" Calum said.

"I tried a lot of things—maybe everything I wanted to try."

"Like what?"

"I don't know."

"Ah, come on. I told you about the handcuffs, and I didn't want to."

"Fine. There was a guy I was seeing. He was like a sexual mentor."

"Are you taking the piss?"

"I never tried leather or any of that stuff. I never thought about it before him, but he showed me all that."

"You're being serious?"

"Of course."

"What did he show you?"

"Bondage, that sort of stuff."

"Did you like it?"

"It was different."

"Good different?"

"It can be fun. There needs to be a lot of trust. I stopped trusting him so it stopped. I haven't seen him for a while."

"For how long?"

"Maybe a month before we met. Something like that." Silence. "It's done though."

"Do you miss doing that stuff?"

"It can be fun, but I like a lot of things."

"Maybe one day you'll show me?"

"Shut up," Michael said, shoving him.

"Don't be nasty. I'm serious. I'll try anything with you."

"You're crazy."

They ate some of the sandwiches, and some strawberries and blueberries Calum bought. They had more beer too and took their shoes and socks off and waded into the water until it reached their knees. Michael joked that they probably shouldn't go any deeper anyway because of the pollution in the lake.

Calum brought four big cans of beer each, all craft beers, and different kinds. It wasn't enough to make Michael feel too drunk, but he was feeling good after the fourth and so was Calum, who was making lots of jokes about them being boyfriends now, and said that since they met, he knew they'd be boyfriends.

They stayed most of the afternoon, and on the ferry back, Calum said he wanted to make Michael dinner, but he needed to get groceries. He apparently made a good lasagna—it was his favourite food—and he wanted Michael to try it, so they took a cab to the supermarket around the corner from his place.

"I'll get what I need for the lasagna and you go pick out a dessert."

"Anything you feel like having?"

"If it has chocolate in it, it'd make me very happy."

Michael went to the frozen section, looking for ice cream. There were four freezers full of it, and every kind of chocolate: dark, white, double, triple. He grabbed a double chocolate one with cookie chunks in it.

He closed the freezer door and turned. Wyatt was standing right behind him, watching him, with a shopping cart full of food. It made Michael jump seeing him.

"I was trying not to scare you," Wyatt said. "I was waiting for you to be done in the freezer."

"You scared me."

"Sorry."

He'd never seen him in public like this, except in the pub when they'd first met.

Wyatt hugged him. "It's good to see you. You look well." He smelled how he always did when he first got out of the shower—like whatever soap he used.

"What are you doing here?" Michael said.

"Shopping."

"No, I mean, it's not close to your place."

Wyatt cleared his throat. "They have parking here. I'm having a dinner party tomorrow. I have a lot of things to pick up."

"You're hosting a dinner party?"

"Tomorrow, yes. My cousin, some neighbours, my boss's daughter and her boyfriend—it's a family dinner," he said.

A "family dinner"? It didn't seem like family to him. The cousin did but the other people weren't family unless they were and he wasn't saying.

"I can't imagine you hosting a dinner party."

"I do it every Sunday."

Wyatt usually wasn't around Sundays, but he never told Michael why until now. They would get together every night but Sunday. Michael thought maybe it had to do with work—getting ready for Monday—but he didn't know it was because of these family dinners.

"We've never had dinner together," Michael said. "I can't imagine it."

Wyatt smiled. "You look good."

"I was at the island," he said. "My shoes are full of sand and I need to shower."

"You like it there, don't you?"

"I guess."

"I remember that."

"What do you mean?"

"When we first met, you said you liked the island. I do listen, more than you think."

Michael forced a smile.

"Well, you look good, even if you need a shower," Wyatt said.

"Thanks."

"You're welcome."

"You look good too," he said, and he meant it but couldn't look at him. Just saying it made him miss being with him—that hadn't changed. Why would it change? He was older but handsome—anyone would think so. Michael had been so mad at him, he forgot about how good he looked—he'd stopped caring how he looked—but seeing him again was a reminder.

"Thank you, Michael," Wyatt said. "You know, I've missed you."

Michael showed him the ice cream in his hand and said, "I gotta go."

"Okay." Silence. "Call me?"

"It was nice seeing you."

Michael went to the self-checkout and paid for the ice cream. He didn't try to find Calum. He texted instead. He said he couldn't find him; he acted like he'd checked everywhere and told him he got ice cream and that he'd wait outside for him.

It was still sunny out and there were lots of people passing by. It was better out there than inside with Wyatt in there.

Calum came out a couple of minutes later carrying two bags. "You better be hungry."

"I am."

"I got a surprise for you too." They walked toward Calum's place. "Aren't you going to ask what the surprise is?"

Michael told himself to smile, so he smiled. "What's the surprise?"

"You're going to have to wait and see." He smacked one of the grocery bags against Michael's thigh.

"What did you get?" Calum asked.

"You're going to have to wait and see."

"Cheeky bugger. I know it's ice cream. You already said."

o

Calum's secret was that he got four different cheeses: a Scottish cheddar and an English one, and two Québécois soft cheeses. He picked up a baguette to eat them with, but it was just a snack since the lasagna was going to take time. They had some wine with the cheese, but Michael was drinking fast. The more he drank, the more he forgot about Wyatt.

Calum opened another bottle of wine when they finished the first. He didn't say anything about Michael's drinking even though he drank a lot more than Calum.

By the time dinner was ready, they were both full on bread and cheese. Michael didn't admit it until Calum said it first. They each had a slice of lasagna anyway, and even though Michael was feeling bloated, he had another half slice because it was really good.

"I'm sending you home with leftovers," Calum said. "Promise you'll reheat it in the oven. It won't taste good if you do it the microwave."

"I promise, you weirdo."

Calum put a movie on after dinner—a documentary about Aretha Franklin he'd wanted to see. They lay across the couch with Calum cuddling Michael from behind. For the first half of the movie, Calum kept putting his hands down the front of Michael's pants. He'd stroke his dick until it got hard, then stop so it'd go back to normal.

Near the end of the movie, when Calum got him hard, Michael rolled over and started kissing him, but then stopped and sat up on top of him.

Calum grinned. "Hello."

"Hi."

Calum slipped his hands under Michael's shirt and rubbed his back. "You're not liking the film?"

"It's okay."

"What do you want to do then?"

"I don't know." He ran his fingers through Calum's hair. "Do you want to try something different?"

"What do you mean?"

"Do you want to try something different? Yes or no?"

Calum laughed and bounced his body a bit, so Michael bounced too. "Aye."

"I want to tie you up."

"Ah, stop talking rubbish."

"I do."

Calum's face turned red and he stopped bouncing. Everything in him got still, but he kept grinning. He was nervous—Michael could tell.

"Didn't you say you wanted me to show you some of the stuff I've done before?"

Calum was quiet.

"Do you trust me?" Michael said.

"Of course I do."

Michael rolled off Calum so they were side by side. "Take your clothes off then."

Calum stood up and grabbed onto his belt but he stopped there and looked confused.

"I said take off your clothes."

Calum undid his belt and pulled his pants down.

"Underwear off too. And the shirt."

Once he was naked, he covered his dick with his hand, acting shy about it, even though Michael had seen him naked a bunch of times.

Michael grabbed a chair from the kitchen and dragged it into the living room. "Sit here," he said. "And no talking until we're done, or I'll go home and you'll have to spend the rest of the night by yourself."

Calum stared at him but didn't move—Michael had never said things like that before.

"I said sit down!"

Calum wiped the chair before sitting. His back was straight and he held onto both sides of the seat like he was worried about falling off.

Michael grabbed Calum's shirt from the floor and wrapped it around his face, covering his eyes and nose. He kept his mouth free, but covered everything else. It was the closest thing he had to a hood, but it worked.

When he was all wrapped up, Michael stood back to take a look at him: he was less like Calum with his face covered up. It made his skin look really white. He had a thin body, no hair, except for his crotch and armpits. His chest, his ass, everything was smooth and white. He could've been anybody with his face covered up like that.

Calum's dick was shifting between his legs with little spasms, until it was hard, standing up straight.

"What is this?" Michael said, grabbing onto it. His voice got deep—it was almost like someone else saying it. "What is this?!"

Calum kept quiet, so Michael came a quarter of an inch from his face. "What is this?" He was breathing onto Calum's lips, making Calum's hands shake.

"Don't move," Michael said. He went to Calum's bedroom and grabbed three ties from behind his door: two solid blue ties and a paisley one. He came back and held them up to show to Calum even though he couldn't see anything.

He used the paisley one to tie Calum's hands together behind his back, looping it through the spindles of the chair. Then he tied his ankles to the legs of the chair with the blue ones, locking him in.

Calum's whole body was shaking now. He was sweating too. His chest was lifting and dropping, and he was moving his head around, trying to figure out where Michael had gone. When Michael touched his chest, he jumped.

"I'm right here," he said. He moved his lips closer to Calum's. "No talking."

He kissed him until the shaking stopped. He kept his hand on his chest to measure the shaking—he found that calming him felt just as good as getting him going.

"It's okay. There's nothing to be afraid of."

He lowered himself down so that he was between his thighs and placed his hands on his calves. "I'm not going to hurt you," he said. "I promise."

10

Michael couldn't stay sleeping because his feet wouldn't stop moving, so he got out of bed. It was three thirty, but he needed to keep moving his feet, so he walked in circles in his bedroom. It didn't help. He went out into the living room and turned the lamp on in the corner.

He couldn't remember how the night ended. Calum was over for dinner, but he couldn't stay. He had a meeting in the morning. Michael remembered that—there were dirty dishes on the coffee table that had dried pasta on them, and some empty wineglasses stained red—but he couldn't remember Calum leaving.

He took the dishes to the kitchen and ran water over them in the sink, while he tried to shake the feeling out of his feet. His stomach was never right when he woke up in the middle of the night either.

Michael put on some coffee and watched it dripping into the pot. Focusing on that helped; it made his feet calm down, seeing the coffee drip.

When it was done, he took his mug to the living room and lay on the sofa. He put a pillow behind his head and was able to go back to sleep.

○

The sun was coming in through the window and shining on his face. It was still early but it was light out. He'd only slept a couple of hours. He lifted his head and looked at the sun through the window. He had to squint to see it, but he got the sudden feeling that the window wasn't big enough. He knew windows couldn't shrink, but it was like it'd gotten smaller. It was big before and now it wasn't. Or maybe the window was always small and he didn't notice.

He looked at the other windows. They'd all shrunk.

The room felt like it was getting smaller too, so he stood up and spun around. It was hard to breathe, and it was as if his heart was going to pop out of his chest. He had to focus to get his breathing under control, trying to do it slowly, going in his nose and out through his mouth.

It was a panic attack; he'd had them when he was a kid. He grabbed onto his neck with both hands and started walking around the coffee table in circles. It was helping him breathe normally, until he got it in his head that he was going to suck all the air out of the room; he was breathing so quickly even though he was trying to go slow, he got it in his mind that it could happen—that the air could be gone if he breathed it all in, so no matter how much he tried to slow it down, he couldn't.

He went to the window, opened it, and hung his head out. He was telling himself that he couldn't suck the air out of the room. It was impossible. He had to keep saying it in his head so he'd believe it.

It was cool out. He closed his eyes and listened to the subtle wind. He kept his head out until his breathing was back to how it was supposed to be. He told himself it was a panic attack. He knew it was a panic attack. He wasn't running out of air.

He pulled his head back in and put some clothes on. He grabbed a heavy jacket from the closet too and went outside. He started walking. He wasn't thinking of where he was going.

It was quiet out. He didn't look at the time, but it was too early for many people to be out. The sun was still rising and the sky was clear. It was cool but nice out. It was good being out. His breathing was fine again.

When he got to Yonge Street, he saw this guy in a shirt that was all ripped up. His jeans were down to his thighs, and he was moving his body in weird ways. It was like he was trying to dance, but there was no music to dance to and he didn't have earbuds in.

When Michael passed, the guy stood up straight and stopped moving. He was making weird faces before but he stopped that too. He was pretending like everything was normal.

He asked Michael for money in a fake accent that sounded like he was trying to be British. Michael said sorry, that he didn't have any money. He didn't check his pockets, but he knew he had nothing.

"You don't have the fuckin' decency to help me, you fuck?" the guy shouted. He wasn't doing the accent anymore, but he kept shouting and started punching the air. Michael had to act like it wasn't a big deal. His breathing was getting heavy again, but if he showed it, he knew it'd make the guy crazier. He kept walking, acting like it was nothing. He didn't look back over his shoulder because he figured it'd make it worse if he did.

Michael wasn't thinking of where he was going—he was try-ing to relax. His breathing was heavy again, and he was moving his feet quickly. When he turned onto Wyatt's street, he wasn't thinking; he was just trying to get his breathing back to normal and it was helping, the closer he got.

Even when he went up to the door and rang the bell, he wasn't thinking either, but the bell sound snapped him out of it. It was like waking up from a dream.

"What am I doing?" he said. He didn't like the sound of his voice. It didn't sound right, and it didn't feel right being there. He didn't mean to go to Wyatt's. He wasn't thinking.

He was standing on his toes, waiting for Wyatt to open the door. He closed his eyes. He thought about being somewhere else. He shouldn't have come. He didn't mean it. He closed his eyes like it'd take him somewhere else.

He thought the door was going to open, but it didn't. Wyatt could've been asleep. He didn't know the time but it was early. The sun was still coming up.

He opened his eyes and moved his head closer to the door, trying to listen inside. It didn't sound like anyone was in there. Wyatt also could've been away for work. He travelled a lot, so he could've been gone.

Michael turned around slowly and walked back down the stairs. He was almost off the lawn when he heard the door open.

"Michael? What are you doing?" It was Wyatt. He was wearing a blue polo that was tucked in on one side and creased on the front. There were marks on his forehead like he'd fallen asleep on something, face-first.

Michael turned. "Hi."

"Can I help you?"

"I was checking on you. I wanted to make sure you're okay."

"Why wouldn't I be?"

"I don't know."

"It's nice of you to check up on me at seven in the morning."

"I didn't plan it. I was just walking."

Silence.

"You okay?" Wyatt said.

"I'm fine."

Wyatt stepped back and pulled the door open. "Come in."

He didn't want to go in, but he was there already, so he walked back up the lawn and followed Wyatt inside.

"Shoes off," Wyatt said, going into the kitchen. "Do you want coffee?"

"Sure."

Michael went to the kitchen and stood by the fridge.

"Sit. You're making me nervous," Wyatt said.

Michael took a seat at the kitchen island. There were crumbs on the counter, so he put his hands on his lap. He didn't think he'd be there again. It was weird but felt good—it was the same excited feeling he used to get when he'd go over.

Wyatt got the coffee going and sat across from him. He ignored the crumbs and put his arms on it. He started saying something, but Michael wasn't hearing it. He looked down at Wyatt's hands. He liked how big they were. The nails were always a bit dirty, but he didn't mind that. They weren't what people would think were nice hands, but that's what he liked about Wyatt—nothing about him was how it should be.

"What about you?" Wyatt said.

"What about me?"

"How are you?"

"I couldn't sleep."

"You look it." He meant it as a joke. He smiled. "I'm not any better. I passed out like this." He pulled at his shirt collar. Michael could smell booze on him. "I'm glad you came. You know I've missed you."

"I missed you too," he said, but it was only because Wyatt said it first.

"You came here because you missed me? I'm flattered."

"I came to check up on you."

"You thought I was dead?"

"No." Michael laughed, then got quiet. Wyatt got quiet too. "Is it weird that I'm here?"

"Yeah, but I'm glad you came. When I saw you at the grocery store a couple of days ago, I didn't think I'd see you again for a long time."

"Here I am."

"Other than not sleeping, you're well?"

"I'm seeing someone."

"Is that right?"

"Yeah."

"Is it serious?"

"I think so."

"That was quick."

Wyatt started asking questions about Calum: who he was, where he was from, and what he looked like.

"What do you mean he's Scottish?"

"He's from there."

"Is he from Scotland or are his parents from there?"

Michael liked that it bugged him; that meant something, to see Wyatt like that. "He's from Scotland. He's been here a few years. He's got an accent and everything."

"You must like that."

"I like a Scottish accent."

"Well, good for you, Michael. That's always what you wanted, isn't it?"

"A Scottish guy?"

"A normal relationship."

"I don't know."

"It's not what you want?"

"I guess it is."

"It sounds like you're not sure."

"We get along."

"I'm happy for you. I've only ever wanted you to be happy, Michael." He got serious. "I mean it. I hope you know that."

"I know. Anyway, what about you?" Michael said.

"What about me?"

"Are you seeing anyone?"

"You know that I don't 'see' people, Michael. That's who I am."

"I know."

"You were never able to accept that. You wanted me to be something I'm not." Wyatt got up to get the coffee. "What do you want in it?"

"I'll have it black."

"See, we are the same." He poured him some. "Maybe I could've done things differently. Did you get my texts or did you block me?"

"I don't know."

"I know you know. I know you better than you know yourself. Do you know how I know?"

Michael couldn't look him in the eye even when he gave him his cup. "Because we're the same?"

"Because we're the same. I was just like you at your age. And you'll probably be like this at my age, lucky you." That made him laugh. Michael laughed too because he wasn't feeling comfortable.

"I was married," Wyatt said. "Did you know that?"

"Yeah, we talked about it."

"He couldn't accept what I am. I didn't tell you that."

"What are you?"

"You know what I am. You've seen it. It's who you are too."

"I wouldn't do what you did."

"What did I do?"

"When that other guy was over and there were the three of us." Wyatt laughed. "You're still not over that, huh?"

"We don't need to talk about it."

"You brought it up."

"I should go. I don't know why I'm here."

Wyatt looked him in the eye. He didn't say anything, he was just staring. Michael liked Wyatt's eyes too. He liked his hands and his eyes. He'd never seen grey eyes like that.

"I'm not a bad person," Wyatt said.

"I didn't say that."

"It's what you're thinking."

"I wasn't thinking that."

"Yes, you were."

"I should go."

"You were too hard on me, Michael." When Wyatt said it, he started crying. It came from nowhere. Michael just watched him because it didn't seem real, but it was real. There were tears coming down his face.

"Look at me. I'm crying," Wyatt said. He tried to laugh, like it'd help. "If you're done with me, I accept that, but please, don't give up on me." He wiped his face. "I don't know why I do the things I do, but I'm not bad. I know I'm not. I care a lot about you." He tried to laugh again. "Can I have a hug?" he begged.

Michael didn't know if he believed Wyatt. He didn't know what to believe, but he hugged him and then he left.

11

Calum was reaching over the car console, grabbing Michael's thigh. "You're quiet."

Michael didn't hear him. He was looking out the window, but his head was somewhere else.

"You're quiet," he said again.

"What?"

"Are you okay?"

"Yeah. Sorry."

"No need to be sorry."

"I was just thinking."

He looked back out the window. It was raining, coming down hard, flooding the roads. Calum was driving slowly, with the windshield wipers swinging back and forth, squeaking against the glass.

"It's hard to see," Calum said.

"Should we turn back?"

"Back home?

"We don't have to go."

He chuckled. "Don't be daft."

"I'm just saying if it's dangerous we don't have to keep going."

"Are you embarrassed by me? You don't want your mother to meet me?"

"Now you're being 'daft.'"

When they pulled up to his parents' place, Michael's mom came out with an umbrella. She must've been waiting by the window.

She went to Calum's side of the car. "It's so nice to finally meet you," she said. She tried to give him a hug, but it didn't work because of the umbrella. Their faces almost smacked together.

She came around to Michael next and kissed him on the cheek. Her face was warm. "I missed him so much," she told Calum. "He's been avoiding us."

"I've just been busy, Mom."

"I know, baby. He's a good boy," she told Calum. She put her arm around him.

"Where's Dad?" Michael said.

"He's working today." She was taking them through the garage. "I'll call him and let him know that you're here."

She already had food out in the dining room. They never ate there. It was usually the kitchen. They'd only eat in the dining room for special occasions. She'd made kibbeh, tabbouleh, kefta in tomato sauce, and warak enab.

His mom took them into the living room and they both sat down.

She disappeared into the kitchen. "How was the drive?" she shouted.

"It was a bit slow. It was very rainy, and there was also some construction."

Calum looked at him from across the living room and winked.

She came out with a tray that had four glasses of soda on it. "There's Diet Coke and 7UP," she said to Calum.

Michael thought Calum might think his mom was some subservient stereotype serving them like that so he said, "Mom, you don't have to do this." He looked at Calum, who didn't seem to mind. He took a 7UP.

"Do what?" She came to him with the tray and looked afraid she'd done something wrong.

"Nothing," he said. He smiled so she smiled with him. "Just sit with us. I haven't seen you in a long time."

She put the tray on the side table and sat next to Calum. "So, you're Irish?" she said.

"Scottish, actually."

"I looked your last name up on the Internet. I've never heard of it before, but it said that it's Irish. I guess the countries are very close."

"Oh. Yes. My great-grandad is Irish, but I was born in Scotland. I am half Irish, you're right."

"I didn't know that," Michael said.

"I'd only been to Ireland twice before my great-grandad died, so I don't feel Irish."

"Did you come to Canada by yourself?" his mom asked.

"I did come, yes."

"Your family must miss you."

"I see them at least twice a year, so it's not bad. I usually go for Christmas, and my parents come during the summer. Sometimes I'll do an extra trip in the spring or fall."

"Why did you leave your home?"

"There aren't the same opportunities there. Not for what I do anyway," he said. "I'm a lawyer. I practice environmental law."

"When I was a little girl, I wanted to be a lawyer." She looked at Michael. "Wallah, I did but the war. I didn't finish school. Is it how it's like on TV?"

The question made Calum laugh. "Sometimes."

His mom started telling him about a British show she was watching on Netflix. It was about criminal lawyers, but she couldn't remember the name of it. Calum knew the one she was talking about. He couldn't remember the name either but said it was a good one; it was the most realistic he'd seen about lawyering, except the third season. He didn't like the third one but said the first two were good.

"Don't tell me anything," his mom said. She grabbed onto his arm and laughed. "I'm on season two."

"I'll keep my mouth shut."

She stopped laughing and looked at her watch. "Are you boys hungry?"

"Aye, Mike said you were making lots of food, so I didn't eat lunch."

"I hope he said good things about my cooking?"

"He said you're a great cook, but that you hate doing it."

"Habibi?" She looked at Michael. "That's not true. It depends on who it's for."

"Um, did you call Dad?" Michael said.

"I did earlier, but he didn't answer. He said that if he's not home in time, we should eat without him, but let me try calling again."

When she went back to the kitchen, Calum mouthed, "Hi."

It made Michael turn red. "Hi."

"I expect a tour of the place; I need to see where my man grew up."

"If you want."

"Of course I want."

Michael tried to smile.

"You're quiet," Calum said. "Is everything okay?"

"I'm fine."

"Are you sure?"

"I'm just trying to get used to this."

James Chaarani's work has appeared in Condé Nast's *Them*, *The Advocate*, *Slate*, and *Vice*. The Toronto, Ontario, resident was selected for Lambda Literary's Writers Retreat for Emerging LGBTQ Voices in Los Angeles.